Contents

Chapter 1. 9

Spencer. 9

Chapter 2. 12

Lennox. 12

Chapter 3. 15

Spencer. 15

Chapter 4. 19

Lennox. 19

Chapter 5. 22

Spencer. 22

Chapter 6. 25

Lennox. 25

Chapter 7. 29

Spencer. 29

Chapter 8. 32

Lennox. 32

Chapter 9. 36

Spencer. 36

Chapter 10. 39

Lennox. 39

Chapter 11. 44

Spencer. 44

Chapter 12. 49

Lennox. 49

Chapter 13. 56

Lennox. 56

Chapter 14. 60

Spencer. 60

Chapter 15. 65

Interrogation. 65

Nibble... 65

Chapter 16. 69

Lennox. 69

Chapter 17. 71

Spencer. 71

Chapter 18. 75

Lennox. 75

Chapter 19. 79

PAPs Nightclub. 79

Lennox. 79

Chapter 20. 86

Spencer. 86

Chapter 21. 91

Lennox. 91

Chapter 22. 94

Spencer. 94

Chapter 23. 100

Lennox. 100

Chapter 24. 103

Spencer. 103

Chapter 25. 106

Lennox. 106

Chapter 26. 112

Spencer. 112

Chapter 27. 120

Lennox. 120

Chapter 28. 126

Spencer. 126

Chapter 29. 129

Spencer. 129

Chapter 30. 133

Lennox. 133

Chapter 31 138

Spencer. 138

Chapter 32. 150

Spencer. 150

Chapter 33. 154

Lennox. 154

Chapter 34. 158

Spencer. 158

Chapter 35. 164

Lennox. 164

Chapter 36. 167

Spencer. 167

Chapter 37. 170

Party. 170

Chapter 38. 175

Crystal. 175

Chapter 39. 176

Spencer. 176

Chapter 40. 179

Spencer. 179

Chapter 41. 189

Lennox. 189

Chapter 42. 193

Spencer. 193

Chapter 43. 196

Lennox. 196

Spencer. 203

Chapter 45. 209

Lennox. 209

Chapter 46. 214

Spencer. 214

Chapter 47. 222

Lennox. 222

Chapter 48. 226

Spencer. 226

Chapter 49. 232

Lennox. 232

Chapter 50.	235
Spencer.	235
Chapter 51.	241
Epilogue.	241
Chapter 52.	246
Jameson.	246

Whitesands' Elite Series (Book 1) Spencer and Lennox's Story.

7 Close friends from 2 Millionaire families each carving out their own paths, relying only on each other and their circle of friendship.

Meet Spencer and Lennox. One hot ex Marine and security businessman and one hardcore farm owner who's past history is not the only thing bubbling to resurface the sexual tension that's built up over a decade of longing is also ready to erupt. From gargoyle one upping, smart mouth come backs and escaping animals, it won't be long before hot lava is spilling over.

Hold on tight for laughter, tears and some serious rides of your life. This is Spencer and Lennox.

Spencer.

10 years ago.

Saying good bye shouldn't have been this hard but to save her from a life of worry, turmoil and fear that I may never make it back THIS was a necessary evil. I know she wanted more. She can't be part of this life. One day she will hopefully understand and forgive me. She will realise my intentions were good and it was from loving her with all of my heart was the reason behind it. Ignoring her cries, as I was driven away, seeing her fall to her knees, head in her hands and rocking on the gravel drive through the rear view mirror seeing her mum holding her tight will always lay heavy on my heart. Jameson, her brother, kept on driving till we were out of sight, only then did I allow myself to hang my own head and started to mentally lock down my own heart. One day she WILL understand.

Lennox.

10 years ago.

Why did he leave me like this? Please Spencer don't leave. I pleaded and pleaded and yet he still jumped in the car with my own brother driving him away. Did he not realise he had my whole heart? Ignoring my cries, I fall to my knees praying the car would turn around and take me with him. He left without even a second glance in my direction. Friends from a young age, families tighter than tight. I thought we had something special. I guess I was wrong. In that moment I swore never to let my heart rule my head, it was time to look after ME. Spencer who? He can leave SO CAN I!

This is our story.

The Whitesands Elite series

Book 1

Spencer and Lennox.

Chapter 1.

Spencer.

Just breathe, in, out, in, out, listening to every sound. Hairs on the back of my neck standing to attention. Laying down on top of the container in a pool of water from the torrential downpour, the wind battering my face as I ready myself to jump. "Stone. He is running straight under you in 3, 2 ,1." Is all I can hear through the earpiece, with my own senses on overdrive I jump, landing directly behind him grabbing his shoulders and pushing him to the floor, he gets up, recon has prepared me for his quick attacks. With his left hand he puts his hand to his belt, pulls out a knife. In one quick movement my hands clip his wrist sending the knife high in the air, jawing him with an uppercut elbow sending him to the ground I grab the knife on its descent and push it deep into his shoulder. "Checkmate Bishop!"

Standing above him pointing my own gun whilst the cavalry arrive, once the rest of Bishops crew were rounded up it was time to open up the wagon. There, in the view of the cartel was the beautiful sight of the biggest drugs seizure to date. I never lose the feeling a win gives me. Bad guys caught, narcotics seized job done. After writing up the reports, standing my men down it was time to head back to Whitesands'.

Reaching the private airstrip I turn on my phone and message the group our code word, the cherubs, they only worry.

ME: Sweet cheeks.

Jameson: Botox,

Maddox: Trout pout.

Donavan: Face lift.

Smiling to myself, I turn it off and board the plane.

"Mr Stone. Welcome back. We are just going over the flight checks and we will be in the air in no time. Your drink is waiting for you at your seat."

"Excellent, Thank you Crystal."

"I have also left you that reading material you were interested in under your seat." She winked, smiled and carried on with her checks. Crystal has been my private hostess for nearly 10 years and mothers me at every opportunity she gets. Only 20 years my senior, I will be forever in her debt. Rubbing the leg she once helped save from a previous mission. She is now a valued member of the team and our eyes and ears on the ground.

Once in the air, I finally relax and look over the material I requested. Opening the envelope, pulling out the papers, smiling so hard my cheeks hurt, I see the most beautiful face that I have tried to forget the last Ten years. Long blond hair, sky blue eyes that sparkle and full lips that have haunted me for years. I lay back, close my eyes and let myself dream of the one and only girl who brought me to my knees. Lennox, and she is back.

Chapter 2.

Lennox.

Driving into Whitesands was a bittersweet moment. Being back with my family meant the world to me, seeing other folk, not so much. Pulling up outside Boyos Bar, I smile to myself seeing my brothers dream come into fruition. He is now finally a chain of his own bars and restaurants, making his way through life and raking in the dough. Me being a silent partner in this little adventure of his has also been a little goldmine for me too. We may come from a wealthy family but we were brought up understanding the value of hard work and money. We may own nearly half of Whitesands but it wasn't a given. We all worked hard to get to where we are. I drag myself out of the hire van and walk into the bar, and there standing in all his glory was my big brother Jameson. Running over to me, picking me up and swinging me around like I was five.

"Your back little sis, I thought you weren't back until tomorrow?"

"Well I got an early start. I like what you have done to the place. It looks even better in person. Face time didn't do it justice."

"I know sis, wait till I show you upstairs. The dance floor is nearly finished, the bar area is nearly completed and the VIP booths are also nearing completion. We should be good to go in little under 2 months." Jameson announced with his cheeky smile.

Running my hands over the solid oak bar rails and the granite bar upstairs looked stunning. lights under the reinforced glass dance floor will be a sight to see when on. Solid oak around the DJ and band area, finishes off the look to a TEE. Once I had the full tour and saw the plans for the kitchen and the terrace area for the restaurant it was time for food.

"I am starved bro, you feeding me today or what?" Smiling and batting my eye lashes, he side eyed me, grinned and pushed me out the door.

"Come on wench, lets feed the help," putting his arm over my shoulder we walked to his car and drove the 5 minutes to Cathie's Cafe. Walking in after all these years, memories flooded back like it was yesterday, the corner booth where we all sat through our youth. Making our way over and sitting in our old places felt a little surreal but I swallowed down the bitter taste and smiled as Cathie virtually ran to the table.

"Let me see you!" Pulling me out from behind the table, eyeing me up and down and spinning me around "Your too skinny, I will sort that out now your back. It's so good to see you again Lenny." with a final hug I managed to escape her claws and sit down. Without even ordering any food a tray of double cheese burger, fries, garlic bread, a portion of onion rings and strawberry milkshake appeared from nowhere.

"Oh she knows me well." I say smiling at Jameson and tucking right in. Jameson laughed at the mixture of food and the dipping of the fries in the milk shake.

"Some things never change little sis," as his phone beeped, nodded, looked back at me, smiled, typed a message and then put it back into his pocket.

"A new girl bro?"

"Nah, just the guys sis."

After Jameson dropped me back at the bar to pick up the van, he followed me home to my new dwellings. Thatcher's Farm. Left to me from our dear Grandpops, he knew how much I loved the place. This is where I belong now. Grandpops knew there would be a time to come back and now was it. I had a taste of the world around us and not all of it was pretty. Working with many animals in foreign countries, learning my trade as I went. One problem, my dwellings are bang next door to my nemesis and close family friend. Spencer. I am ready to face the next chapter of my life, hopefully the old life won't catch up with me and Spencer. Well, he can stay well clear if he knows what's best for him!

Chapter 3.

Spencer.

Walking through the door, turning off my alarm I head straight to the bedroom. Throwing my bag on the bedroom floor I go into the bathroom turn on the shower, strip off and climb into the cubicle. Placing both my hands on the shower wall letting the hot water hit the back of my neck and spray down my back only then do I start to relax. Washing away the stress of the mission, I clamber out of the shower, fall onto the bed were sleep finally finds me.

What is that noise? Waking from a peaceful slumber.

Bang, bang, bang, "Ouch you little fecker. THAT'S IT! You're going down!" is all I can hear. Dragging my arse off the bed and over to the window, all I can see the most beautiful sight, Lenny trying to knock down the post that is clearly in her way. Her hair tied up in a messy bun, blue tank top and matching shorts wearing the worlds brightest wellington boots ever to be worn. Raising her right knee she drop kicks the post. I smile watching the scene, "Oh this is going to be fun!"

Quickly brushing my teeth, grabbing a pair of shorts and fling my trainers on I head out back.

"Excuse me, do you mind keeping the noise down, people are trying to sleep?" Lenny stopping mid kick and turns, looks me dead into the eye, oh how I have missed those eyes.

"HMMM, how about no so why not turn around and fuck off before I drop kick your sorrowful arse."

"Is that before or after that post wins? Just so I know and can prepare myself to run for cover. How have you been Lenny?"

"It's Lennox. None of your damn business."

"Oh I think you may find it is." With a wink and smile I made my way back into the house.

Shouting after me, "You lost that right years ago Spencer. Now go and crawl back under the rock you just came back from and leave me alone."

Going over to the coffee machine and popping in a pod I hear my phone beep.

Maddox: BBQ at mine 12'o'Clock, don't be late bitches.

Me: Count me in,

Jameson: Me too,

Donavan: I'll be there.

Me: Need to go and see the folks first, I maybe late,

Maddox: No sweat. See you when you land.

Setting the phone down I hit the shower before heading over to mam and dads. Pulling up on the driveway the door opening before I walk up the steps,

"Good morning Mr Stone. Welcome back. Your parents are out on the veranda, can I fetch you anything?" asked the butler,

"Coffee please Phillip,"

"In an instant Sir." Handing me a water pistol as if it's an everyday occurrence. Walking out on the veranda I hear the laughter before I see the chaos, the folks with super soakers drenching each other. Even after all of these years they still feel young at heart and still think they're living their youths. "Hey guys my turn," with several pump actions I aimed and fired. Three of us running round trees, behind benches and wherever else we could find cover, they never forget how to have fun and just let loose. Always trying to one up one another, I dare say this has mam written all over it.

Leaving the folks and heading to Maddox's I pull up at the gated entrance, tapping in the code and I slowly made my way to the parking bays, it doesn't take long to hear the party is in full swing. Grabbing the case of beer from the boot I make my way up to the house. Punching in the door code I let myself in and through the house I follow the noise. Once outside you see a 15 metre swimming pool smack bang in the middle of the grounds, bbq cooker to the right corner cooking up the steaks, chicken and sausages, music blasting from the speaker system and our group sat on the decking. Opening the box and putting the bottles in the coolers, which is more like an ice cooler bin I give people a way and sit down and join in with the conversation. With my back to the wall, I guess old habits die hard, I took my time in looking around. Seeing a few girls throwing a beach ball in the pool trying to be noticed, a few more in their bikinis playing table tennis with a few local lads and there in full view of everyone was Lenny playing fucking swing ball with Caitlin. I guess she never rid herself of her anger issues from this morning post fight. As if she sensed me, she stopped, squared her shoulders tilting her head a little to the side and then carried on. Oh yes, she knows I am here. I stare and soak up the sun.

"How's the bar coming along Jammy?" I ask Jameson,

"Looking good. You need to come and see it now your back and pick up some tools and help. It has changed a lot since the last time you seen it."

"Can't wait, when's opening night?"

"Yeah Jammy! When IS opening night?" A desperate Donavan asks.

"A little under 2 months I reckon Donna," earning him a punch in the arm,

"Stop calling me fucking Donna Dickwadd,"

"Nah it suits you," all of them falling about laughing,

"Fuck off. I will cut my hair when I win the bet!"

" Fuck sake, how long has this shit been going on now?"

"Two years and I am winning the fucker,"

"Your bets go on far too long, just cut it already Donna," That earned us the birdie as we fall apart, clutching my side and wiping my eyes. Yes great being back.

Chapter 4.

Lennox.

I felt him walk in even before he opened his mouth. A full body shiver, that only happens when he is close by even though I thought I buried it deep, I guess it has a mind of its own and never listens' to my opinion. I stopped hitting the ball, squared my shoulders and tilted my head to see if I could hear what he was saying. Even after all of this time he still manages to have an effect on me. I throw the ball in the air and smack it as hard as I can picturing his face on it. If he thought this was going to be all about him, think again, these are my friends and family too and if he thinks he can plant himself back into my life he can think again. Cordial I will be but that the line and that fucker will never be crossed. Walking over to the cooler I take out two bottles, uncap them and walk back over to Caitlin, handed her a bottle, tapped rims and sat by the pool.

"I didn't think he would be back this early Lennox, I am sorry."

"Not your fault Caitlin. We are all in the same group and run the same circles that will never change. He maybe your brother and I will be polite, I am just shocked to see him back as he will be of me."

"He has been back a while Lennox."

"A while?" Curiosity getting the best of me,

"Yeah, came back a year ago, no one told you?"

"I guess I missed that memo."

" He still has time away as his business has security firm dictates him to, however, he is pretty much at home 75% of the time. He has put the security in place at Boyos Bar, has Jameson not told you?"

"No, I guessed I missed that memo too."

"SHIT. I am sorry Len. I thought you were aware if I knew you didn't know I would have told you myself. Mind you his security guys look scary as hell but I guess they have to in that kind of business."

"Hmmmm. I need the bathroom, fancy grabbing us some food whilst I am gone?"

"No problamo."

Placing my drink on the poolside table I head inside, the downstairs bathroom being engaged I head upstairs. Reaching the top I can't help over hearing Spencer on his phone.

"Hey doll how's you? Anytime you want me you know that day or night. See you then. Alright beautiful give me an hr. By Crystal."

Quickly closing the bathroom door I did my business and hoped he had walked back downstairs. I won't lie, my heart twanged a little knowing he was talking sweet talk to another woman. I walked out on to the hall and straight into a wall of Spencer. Stood stock in front of me. Looking up into his deep brown eye I gave him my most hatred stare, my arms crossed over my chest and gritted out,

"Move!"

"No."

"MOVE!"

"NO."

"What do you want Spencer I haven't time to play this game with you?"

"The bathroom. Can you please stand aside?"

Side stepping and leaving a clear path for your royal highness to gain entry leaving him there with his smug look I retreat down the stairs and out of his view. Angry with myself for letting him get under my skin I wait patiently to pull it back. Hearing him come back to the party I stand from the pool strip off my top and shorts and show my new skimpy yellow bikini, I turn and dive into the pool without even a sideward glance. Caitlin quickly follows coming up for air and laughing I turn to see him saying something to Jameson, glaring back at me with a face like thunder he storms out. 1 - 0 to me arsehole. Game On!

Chapter 5.

Spencer.

I could see her reflection through the bedroom mirror listening to my conversation. Crystal already hanging up, she thinks Crystal is my new toy. She is making this fun far too easy.

"Hey doll how's you? Anytime you want me you know that day or night. See you then. Alright beautiful give me an hr, by Crystal." Her face dropped and anger rose she quickly stormed into the bathroom. Waiting outside the door I can't help laughing to myself. She comes out of the bathroom and not looking where she was going ran smack into me.

"Move!"

"No."

"MOVE!"

"NO!"

"What do you want Spencer? I haven't time to play this game with you."

"The bathroom. Can you please stand aside?"

So easy ruffling her feathers she takes off downstairs and leaves me smirking.

Walking outside smiling to myself I stop dead right next to Jameson watching the movie unfold in front of me. Lenny was stripping off her clothes. Who the fuck said this was a good idea. It was bad enough her taking her top off but the sexy wiggling of her arse and hips stepping out of her shorts was another level. Yellow, fucking YELLOW bikini. Is she deliberately trying to piss me off? I have a good mind to go over there, fling her over my shoulder, smack her arse and drive her home. She turned and dove into the pool, quickly followed by Caitlin. Glaring at her "Comicon." is all I needed to say to Jameson, "Flash," was his reply. Jameson, Donavon and Maddox clanked bottles together as I turn and storm out. THIS will be revisited at a later date Fucking yellow, she knows war has been declared.

Down the pier of Whitesand beach I sit on a two way seat looking out to the sea, peace and tranquillity came over me when Crystal comes and sit beside me."How does it feel to be home boss?"

"Bliss, however, I feel war is going to be declared with my neighbour soon." Both laughing as we both know whom I am talking about.

"Does she know you know?"

"NO. Not yet. The least she knows the better. We can control the situation easier this way. I don't want her forcing things or running. It needs to stop and now I am on my own turf it will be easier."

"Right you are boss. I have put a detail on her and her families homes. Cameras in areas that are hidden. We need her out of her house for at least 24 hours to sort out trip switches and alarms around her home. Can you sort that?"

"Yes. I will let you know when the coast is clear to carry out anymore maintenance work. I will let Jameson know that I am putting in security at the house as he wants her safe living on her own. Sit tight and I will be in touch. In the meantime tell Topez to hide better, I saw him earlier and if I can spot him then others might."

"Will do Mr Stone."

"For goodness sake woman, will you call me Spencer already instead of boss or Mr Stone. Fucksake."

Earning me a clip across the head, "No!" and with a genuine smile Crystal stood up and walked away leaving me listening to the soft waves of the sea washing up to shore and out again. Missed this too.

Me: Heading back home. Catch up tomorrow.

Jameson: All good?

Me: Cracking. Need to have access for 24 hours, can you sort?

Jameson: No problem, just let me know when.

Me: See you tomorrow.

Driving home and all I can think about is Lenny and that fucking bikini! Pulling up onto the drive way my phone buzzes alerting me that Lenny is on her way home. Smiling to myself time to dance baby. Putting everything in place I wait eagerly for her to reach home. Hearing her car pull up and going into the house I start the action. Putting on my favourite band and feeding it through the speaker system, I casually walk outside into my garden. I feel her eyes on me there's no need to turn to make sure. I just know I am being watched that tingle she always gives me is on hyper alert. Standing next to the hammock I grab the back of my t-shirt from behind my neck and pull it in one motion over my head and throw it onto the chair. Knowing she can see all of me, I lay my arse down in the hammock with a beer in one hand and the other laid behind my head I simply let myself swing.

Chapter 6.

Lennox.

Hearing the music blaring from his garden, I look out the bedroom window and there he was taking his top off and laying on his man swing. I needed to steady myself and hold the ledge. Ripped like a Greek God and his V dipping under his shorts like big neon arrows saying look at me, pure perfection. All I needed was to open a can of diet coke and watch the show and explode. I swore I would never let this happen to me again. I wouldn't let him under my skin. I stood there and watched to what felt like minutes when he got out of his man swing, looked up at me, how did he know where to look? Putting up his two index fingers showing 1-1 he winked at me smiled and went inside. The BASTARD is onto me. Fuck! I can't help denying how turned on he makes me. That body needs putting away and never letting out EVER AGAIN!

Waking up in a bad mood was all Spencer's fault. His hot body of a temple God and an arse that was far too good to be legal, kept me awake tossing and turning all night. The only time I had some relief was when I caved in and had to get off to the images of the Greek God himself. Locating my box of hidden treasures from in the closet, I found my favourite bunny Bugs and reacquainted ourselves. Picturing Spencer in his man swing, straddling over him, Spencer gripping my thighs and matching me bounce for bounce thrust for thrust taking me to heights never before reaching, licking his thumb he stroked my clit and that's all it took to take me over the edge. My fantasies of Spencer are going the be a real problem. I can just tell.

When sleep finally found me it wasn't long before I woken by whatever godly machine I was hearing. I drag my carcass out of bed to the window. "Are you fucking kidding me!" I grab my robe, tying it as I bolt downstairs and outside.

"OI. DICKWADD! You taking the piss? It's not even half seven in the morning and you're on your granddad grass machine, couldn't it have waited till nine? It's Sunday for goodness sake!"

"I am sorry what? I can't hear you."

"Turn it off then!"

"Sorry?" Putting his hand behind his hear.

"TURN IT OFF THEN!"

" Hold on. I will turn it off. Now tell me again Lenny, Do you want to borrow my machine? Well Yes you can but it comes with a price."

"NO! I don't want to borrow your granddad machine. I want you to stop using you beard trimmer till a reasonable time, seven thirty in the morning IS NOT A REASONABLE TIME!"

"AHHH Lenny, Lenny, Lenny, You know the early bird catches the worm,"

"Yeah well, anymore shit this early and you will be laying in the ground WITH the worms Dickwadd!"

"Would you like a coffee?" In his arrogating voice,

"No. I want sleep."

"Breakfast?"

"No, SLEEP!"

"Help with the garden are?" wiggling his eyebrows,

 "Fuck no - SLEEP ARSEHOLE SLEEP!"

"If you want to sleep with me Lenny just ask." Placing his hands palms up either side of his shoulders.

How fucking dare he, fuming and ready to blow a gasket in his face.

"I want to go back to bed WITHOUT YOU and sleep so can you just KEEP OFF YOUR SHAVING MACHINE TILL NINE 'O' FUCKING CLOCK!"

"No!"

"Pardon?"

"No! You haven't said please. Now that's just bad manners and I know Barbara and Geoff taught you those." Smirking at him.

"PLEASE stop talking, Please stop cutting the grass and PLEASE WEAR SOME FUCKING CLOTHES!" With that, I turn to leave and walk back into the house when he grabs my wrist spins me round back to him being right up in my face.

"Now, was that so hard?" Hovering over my lips by millimetres he lets go of my wrist turns on the machine and as he is driving it into his outhouse I can't let him have the last word. That's just not happening I turn and shout "DO NOT BREAK MY GARGOYLE WITH THAT HAIR TRIMMER EITHER!" Walking away all I could think of was how I hoped he would have bent me over the mower, smack my arse and taken me there and then. Only problem is, I can't forgive him for what he did to me and even if I could forgive and forget. I can't get close. I won't be able to survive a second dose of Spencer heartbreak. He won't be able to look at me in the same light anyway if he ever found out.

Chapter 7.

Spencer.

Not liking how she is making me feel, I needed to walk away before I did something I would regret. I wanted to fuck her right there and then but it will have to wait. For now. I need to be on my game if I am to keep her safe. Fucking the only woman I have ever loved will simply just have to wait. Going inside I quickly showered and headed out. Driving out of the grounds I stop and get out of the SUV and smile at Gordon the Gargoyle I take out the hippy rainbow coloured wig I bought yesterday from the front seat and place it on his head. Tapping the side of its face I smile.

"See you soon Gordon," and drive off. Meeting up with Jameson at Boyos we were going over the security plans for the up and coming opening and securing the place. We also went over the plans to secure Lenny's house.

"So, When can you get her away for a day?"

"As soon as your ready to move, has there been any movement yet?"

"A little, they are following the breadcrumbs we left so hopefully they won't be too far. Just need all we have in place by then. I STILL can't believe she was in there when this went down. Why does she always end up in the wrong place at the wrong time?"

"I don't know. She always liked getting into the thick of it when we were kids, something's never change I guess. How could she be so stupid!" Jameson looked at me seeing the frustration there.

"She always knew you would be there to save her I guess Stone."

"Shit!" Rubbing my head in my hands I can't believe I nearly lost her. She needed her to be away from all of this.

"What was she trying to prove? She didn't even know this was happening or that I would be there. How can she have?"

"You trained her well to get out of scrapes like this. Even if she didn't know it was you in the back ground. Turner did well in the training at least we know she can handle herself if push comes to shove."

"Yeah but I never want her in that situation again. It nearly killed me off the last time." Worry across both of our faces was evident. We need this shit sorting once and for all.

"Right, you get her out this weekend and we will finish off the triggers and last security video cameras in place."

"I will send her and Caitlin to a spa retreat for the day. Knowing them two, they will pack for an overnight stay too. I will think up something to get them there no worries."

"Great. Now let's see what we need to do."

After the meeting with Jameson I drove to the office to finalise what I needed and looked through the Intel we gathered on the surveillance tapes and I studied every move. Familiarising myself with the one person I thought I saw the last of. This time he won't live to see another day, as soon as he makes his move I will be there and my face will be the last thing he ever sees. I just wish we had a clear picture of him. Balaclava's on every picture isn't making it any easier. Anger over took me and I headed through the back to the gym and fighting area and met the team.

"Right guys let's do this. Turner and Jack bag work. Topez and Sinner your with Nibble and myself floor work lets fight."

For two hours we rotate and go through fight moves, restraints, escapes holds and fighting scenarios. We learn 'Banners' moves to a fine art and how to turn them around on them. When they arrive, we will be ready, waiting and raring to go.

Chapter 8.

Lennox.

Driving out to see Caitlin I slam the breaks on. "What on earth?" Then it hit me. Spencer! Giggling to myself I placed the scarf I had on the backseat in case of emergencies around Gordon's neck. I nicknamed him Gordon when I first saw him when grand pops lived here. I used to always climb over him and talk nothing but shit. Gordon knew all of my secrets and was an amazing listener. Tying the scarf securely I drove off to gym, time to work these muscles till they're so sore my head forgets all about Spencer. Walking into the gym I spot Caitlin is already here, I go over to the running machines and start on a steady walk and warm up slowly.

"Hey Caitlin. Sorry I am late. I had a Gordon moment."

"Yeah what did Gordon say today?"

"He has a new hair doo, a lovely rainbow coloured wig, I dare say from Dickwadd so I have completed the ensemble with a scarf. If he wants to mess with Gordon then he won't win that charade!"

"I am loving how you two just slide straight back into your little tug of war games must be making you all warm inside." With a very big grin on her face I could tell Caitlin is LOVING the shit show. "Nah, he just needs putting in his place."

"Hey, I was actually going to ask you if you have any plans this weekend?"

"Not that I know of why you ask. Want to do something?"

"WELL DEAREST FRIEND. I have 2 all day passes to Spa Luxury this weekend. I just think a nice girlie time wine, food, lay about on loungers, back massages, facials the works. You in?"

"Hell Yes I am. What time we allowed in from?"

"Eight am, however, I need to take care of a few errands first so how about I pick you up about 9?"

"Thanks Caitlin you're a legend. It's just what the Dr ordered. It just so happens I need a waxing so all over that I am it's saves two trips."

"You want to head out for some food Lenny?"

"Not right now, thanks though, I am going to go and spar a little, need to release some of this adrenaline,"

"Spencer adrenalin you mean?" With a wink she left and I made my way to the ring. Leg and foot protectors on, hand wraps and mitts, secure head guard at the ready as well as my mouth guard, I need this frustration gone I aren't sore enough and I need a release and I need to forget all about Stone. He is consuming my every thought, movement and even dreams, I cannot escape this man. Since coming back he has never left my head and it is time he was gone.

"Lenny you're up," putting on the head guard and putting in the mouth guard I turn and slide through the ropes. I head to the centre of the ring and there he is, in his full glory sporting a HUGE grin. My nemesis and dream hogger. Spencer. Fucksake I cannot catch a break.

"Let's dance Lenny, your arse is mine." With his trademark wink and blowing a kiss my way I quickly punch him in the groin and he goes down,

"Fine let's dance, but are we starting with the worm?" Next minute I hit canvas after he swiped my calf's and I dropped.

"Nice move Lenny, but I know your game," I roll onto my shoulders and front flip to stand, taking my stance and motion Spencer to get up.

"Bring it!" Is all I needed to say. He right hooks and I dip move right and hit his ribs on the way up and move out. He comes at me with a front kick, I elbow down round house and move round, he counter kicks to my head,

I dodge again and try to take out his left knee. He sees the move and jumps over, he lands a one, two and I counter back. I go for the solar plexus but he reads it pretty well, which is good for me. He catches my foot I jump up swing my body round and back kick his jaw, he instantly releases the foot but even I know he is humouring me. Well not today. I was in my rhythm when he counters swipes me again but I wasn't quick enough to see it coming I hit the canvas.

"Come on Lenny, anyone could see that coming," He holds his hand out to help me up. I take it then drag him down to me, placed both feet on his thighs then flip him he lands rolls grips me in a floor hold.

"What you going to do Lenny? THINK? How do you get out of this hold? Come on you know it THINK!" Quickly take off the gloves I take my two index fingers place them behind his ears and push in and up, he instantly releases the hold and I am worn out on the canvas heaving.

"Good. You remembered quite a lot from the old days and a few new moves too. Well Done!"

"How did you know I can still fight?"

" Well for one, I showed you when we were young and two you never forget." Getting right up close to me face still on the canvas.

"Also, Jameson said you have kept up with training since you left. Where did you train?"

"Oh here and there. I needed to."

"Why?"

"I just did alright Spencer!" For a fleeting moment anger showed in his eyes and him this close to me wasn't a good idea.

"Why Lenny? What has you so worked up?"

"Besides you? None of your business Spencer so leave it." As I moved to get to my feet he pulled me back down, straddled me and pinned my hands above my head.

"Tell me."

"NO." he came closer.

"Tell me!"

"No," feeling his lips close to my ear.

"Tell me why Lenny."

"No."

"Why not?"

"Because I can't." My eyes starting to water as his lips descended on me. My own having a mind of their own matched the urgency. Slipping his tongue inside my mouth and danced with my own, it was perfect and passionate. As quick as it started he stopped. Looked me in the eyes.

"This conversation isn't over baby!" Before he could get up I thrust upwards, catching him unawares and knocking him over my head. I jump up look down and smile.

"Oh but it is!" I turn, slip through the ropes and walk back to the changing rooms only hearing the laughter coming from the ring. With a smirk on my face I leave him laying there.

Chapter 9.

Spencer.

Watching her sassy arse leave the gym to the changing rooms I quickly adjusted my shorts finally stopping the laughter I couldn't contain I gather my thoughts and head to the showers. Lenny not knowing my business is attached to the gym, I could see her through the two way mirror when she entered. She went straight over to Caitlin on the treadmills where they ran for about an hour. I could see her moving over to the ring when I quickly left through the side door that only my team knows exists and went straight to the ring. Dismissing Henry, who was already there to spar, fighting with her was a dream, she knew I was going easy on her. I needed to see what she had to offer and what I can help with. I need her to be sharp and retaliate without questioning it. I couldn't help but straddle her and kiss her. I knew it was coming I couldn't help it she is like a magnet force field. Walking into the showers I put on the cold high power strip off and stand under the shower head. Gripping my cock I start imagining her underneath me, kissing me with her hands moving up and down my back and finger nails digging into my shoulders. I move down her body licking around each nipple and hearing her moans. Gripping my hair she pushes my head down towards her clit.

"Lick that!" She whispers. Taking it between my teeth and lick around the ball of nerves she climaxes grips her legs together locking me there. I grip my cock harder in a rhythm of its own and cum hard finally having the release I so badly craved. I rest my head against the shower wall and gather myself before I wash off I get out the shower, dress grab my bag and walk out just in time to see Lenny pull out of the car park. Smiling to myself I unlock my car before seeing a green SUV pull away from the kerb and follow Lenny. I quickly jump in turn the engine on bang it I first gear and swerve off the gravel and onto the road. I make sure I am two cars behind Lenny and the Green SUV. I punch in the speaker phone Crystals number.

"Hey boss. What's..." Before she could even finish the sentence I tell her Green SUV and licence plate and run it ASAP.

"It's a rental boss, under the name of Smith."

"How ironic. Is it fitted with a tracker?"

"Yes but it has been turned off. Want me to try and override it?"

"That goes without saying. Let me know when it's done. Also, I placed a device on Lenny's car too is it in operation yet?"

"Yes boss. If your tailing ease back the might notice you."

"Who's the boss man here Crystal?"

"Well it's up for debate boss," With that I laugh and end the call, I ring Jameson.

"Hey, Tom and Jerry,"

"There in ten Spike." For years we have always made references to certain things in our lives. Our own code we lived by that only we understood. Jameson knew instantly Tom and Jerry was the cat and mouse game we play when troubles at the door and Spike is me, the killer dog waiting to bite. Sinners pulls behind me to carry on following the SUV. It seems to have tailed away from Lenny. I maybe wrong about the occupancy of the vehicle. It has been known. Once. However, something is telling me not this time. They are here and they will be doing their own surveillance work. Let's play boys. With that I pull up at the security base and in follows Maddox, Jameson, Donavan alongside Topez, Turner, Nibble and Jack. Crystal has everything ready for us as we all pile into the recon room. Bolting down the door and securing the soundproof room we get down to business.

Chapter 10.

Lennox.

The week has dragged, after the kissing situation and many nights getting myself off to the image of him taking me in the ring and tying me to the ropes so he can take what he wants. I have hardly slept. Thank goodness it is the weekend. A car beeps out front of the farm house and I instantly know it is Caitlin, listening to clanking of her suspension is a big give away. She really does need that looking at. I grab my bag and head out. Jameson is coming over later to check the fault in the lights, I was going to ask Spencer but the further away from me he is the better. I lock up and jump in Caitlin's car.

"Let's go, go, gooooooo!" I turn and look at Caitlin who cannot stop laughing,

"What's up with you all laughing and giggly?"

"Ohhh you will know soon enough." I tell her to stop as soon as we clear the end of the drive. Spencer has placed a witches nose over Gordon's and has tied it behind so it doesn't fall off. Caitlin still laughing at my expression. My jaw open I shake my head and look at Caitlin who is crying with laughter.

"Have you helped with this?"

"No. I have just arrived but your face Lennox your face!" Tears flowing down her cheeks and uncontrollably laughing, I turn and growl.

"That bastard is going to get it!" I jump back into the car thinking of what I can put on poor Gordon next. I will not let it spoil my day.

"STOP! Take me back to the house!" Remembering the elf costume I have from a fancy dress party I not long went to. Caitlin reversed up the drive as I practically fall out of the car I ran into the house and up the stairs. Head to the far wardrobe in the bedroom find the costume grab the ears and run back down the stairs. I stop dead in my tracks. I sense something is off. Didn't I close that door before I left? I turned into the kitchen and tried the door. It was locked. Turning I walk out. Once back in the car Caitlin notices something is amiss.

"What's wrong?"

"Nothing. I could have sworn I closed the kitchen door it was open when I went back in. I checked the back door and it is locked but I am SURE I closed it. I always close the doors!"

"Are you sure I did beep and you ran straight out."

"Yeah maybe," With a shrug of my shoulders we drove back out of the drive stopping at Gordon. Placing the ears onto his already rather large stone ones we leave for Spa Luxury trying to shake off this feeling of nervousness. I definitely closed that door. I guess the jitters still surface now and again.

Pulling up outside of the spa we jump out of the car and head onside whilst the valet parks up. Signing in we go off to get changed for our relaxing day. First up waxing, I haven't let myself go by no means but intimate area is in needs of a good seeing too. In more way than one. It's been a while. After the meadow has been sorted, it was off to the massage tables. Laying down on opposite tables our masseuses instruct us to lay front forwards, arms by our sides and relax.

"AHHHH Bliss!" whispers Caitlin.

"I hear you sister." I groan.

"You happy your back Lenny? You seem a little distracted?"

"Yeah just old ghosts I guess. I can't wait for the animals to come to the farm and give me a purpose. I miss being around them, the feeding, fussing help delivering youngens."

"The mucking out, biting, runaway, falling on and in shit, yeah sounds glamorous!" With a giggle. Caitlin loves it when fuss over animals, she always said its easier for her to have her fill of all the cooing over the baby animals than it is to actually own a pet. "Which ones you having first?"

"I need a dog first. Guard dog so maybe a border collie to help work the animals as well as guard. However, it all depends on what the rescue centres have."

"Yes and you are TOTALLY going to leave with just one. You're a walking billboard for waifs and strays," laughing at me.

"You know I can't help it. It's my thing, it's what I do. I can't see animals suffering and kicked to the kerb all because they have something wrong with them. They didn't ask for three legs, one ear and missing teeth. All animals deserve a home and I am in a position to help offer one. It's why grand pops left me the farm. He knew my love for animals was just as powerful as his own. It is a good fit."

"When are you starting work on the farm? Some parts still look good. Will it need much work?"

"No, not really. Grandpops kept it pretty maintained and Donavan always came round to keep it up to standard so no worries on that level. It just needs a good clean out and some animals."

"What type you able to take in?"

"The usual, cats, goats, sheep, pigs and whatever else I can smuggle in." giggling away to myself.

"You are the Mother Teresa of the animal world." laughing a loud. "ERRR Lenny?"

"Yes?"

" Sorry I didn't tell you about Spencer being back and I am sorry we kind of lost touch there for a while. You seemed to vanish from the radar. You had us worried for a time there."

Stiffening up I turn my face the other way hiding my own expression.

"It's alright. You know what it is like in the middle of a rain forest, you can't exactly find a signal or use a landline but we are back together again now so you were worried over nothing. thanks for caring though" Maybe one day I will be brave enough to tell her my story on how I tried to stop animal abduction and trade and how it nearly killed me when I finally realised what was happening. I still have no idea who it was that saved my stupid arse from being killed in the cross fire. One minute I was kneeled on the floor with a knife to my neck being cut for kicks to people being shot around me and taken to a hospital and left. I woke up 3 days later with Jameson sat by my bedside. I have no idea how he knew I was there. Possibly from my ID emergency kit but I was thankful for him being there. Maybe one day I will go back and try and find the group who saved me. Highly unlikely.

As the masseuse moved my hair to one side I flinch and she instantly stopped and removed her hands.

"I am so sorry Miss. I didn't mean to make you jump. I was just moving your hair from the oils. I apologise." In a shaken voice.

"It's fine. I am sorry if I scared you. Just to the shoulder blades will be fine and leave the neck is that alright?"

"Yes. That is fine. Sorry again."

Caitlin looking very confused. "You alright Lenny? What was that about?"

"Oh nothing. I was in a world of my own and jumped a little that's all."

"No neck massages? You loved those once over." With a questioning look.

"I know but things change I guess." With that I turn back to Caitlin, "Honestly I am fine," with a smile I then close my eyes and try and think of happier times.

"Hey Lenny, Did you bring clothes for the evening meal?"

"I diiiiiiiiid. What time we booked in to eat? I also brought an overnight bag JUST IN CASE we decided to stay." With a smile on my face. Forced but still there.

"Oh My Gosh. YES I did too. Great minds you see girl and it just so happens I booked us a suite so we can stay. It was my home coming treat for you." Smiling broadly you can tell she was so proud of herself for going the extra mile to keep us out like she did when we were kids. Granted it was only sleep over's where she would theme a night and have everything ready for us. She looks like the cat that caught the cream.

An hour soon passed, we made our way to the restaurant bar and ordered some snacks to have by the private pool. Pure bliss. Out in the blazing heat we relaxed into the day and didn't move till we made our way to our suite to get ready for the evening.

Chapter 11.

Spencer.

"Fuck, that was close." Whispering to the guys from the ear piece as I hid in the larder. As if she came back in. "For fucks sake, she nearly found me cuddling the baked beans. What a sight that would have been for her. Shocked by a Baked Beans hugger."

I let out a deep breath, made my way out and unlocked the back door to let in the crew. Jameson too pressure pads under the carpets for the doors. Topez rewired the motion sensors that were already in place but upgraded to cameras inside and heat source. I took care of the rest. Check all windows and fitted them with sensors for opening and shutting from the outside, door security and pressure pads up the stairs. Access to underneath the floor boards was why she needed to be gone for 24 hours we needed to rip up the carpets and floorings. All access required. When these guys come around we will be waiting and ready for them. Topez and Sinner took on the out houses and fitted cameras and sensors for every possible angle. NOTHING is getting in or out of this place without us seeing it first. Everywhere was fitted with a visual of the room, besides the bathroom and bedroom. They have trigger sensors not video. I wouldn't sleep ever again if her room had those in. Would have 24 hour access to my very own sex room viewing. Note to self. Must remember to buy the popcorn at the next shop visit. Four hours into the whole rewiring Crystal came with food supplies. Outside in the paddock we sat down to eat.

"Thanks for this Spencer, I always sleep better at night knowing your close her." Jameson says sombrely,

"I told you she will always be my first priority."

"She nearly got you killed or did you forget that little detail?"

"Well for starts she didn't know it was my team and I and secondly, I never nearly died that's a bit extreme." laughing at him.

"Really. So you nearly losing your leg wasn't a near death experience?"

"NAAAAAAH, cut myself worse shaving mate." Laughing.

"Would that be with a machete then?" falling off a log with laughter but still seeing the point and not the one on a knife.

"I would do it all again in a beat you know that!"

"Boys. let it rest. The legs fine and Lenny is home safe and sound and you have made new friends with baked beans so alls good." laughs Crystal, with rub on my shoulder as she walks past to sit on a large tyre, "But if you start farting in the office, you can clean the room yourself!" and with that we all fell about laughing, all seriousness vanished and banter in its place. Working long into the evening all work finished it was time to load up and check all is in working order. Jack had been uploading the software onto the computer network of the security system. Connect it up to the work devices of mobiles and I Pad's we were out of there, carefully putting the place back to how it was and closing that all infamous back kitchen door. Saying a quick goodbye to my new baked bean friends I left and headed home for a shower. Meeting back up with the guys for food at one of Jameson's restaurants 'THE BROTHERS' This was Jammies first one he opened many moons ago. His high end food for decent prices and no cutting corners, he has made it a 5 Star Michelin restaurant where people come from miles around to sample the delicious offerings. My boyo has done good. Meeting in the private booth that's always reserved for us I drop my arse down and the waitress was already heading our direction with our drinks. No need to order they already know it. Ordering our food and talking shite my phone beeps alerting me to a message. Normally in company, I would ignore it as my boys are all here, however this is a beep tells me that it is work related incoming call. I take my phone out and tap in the code then use face recognition and then thumb print I see it is from Nibble. I slide to answer,

NIBBLES: Green SUV pulled up boss outside. Two men about to enter. 5ft10 medium build, dark hair, buzz cut, scar face, jeans and blue T-shirt packing ankle holder right foot left hander, other male 6ft 1, blond hair, larger frame, checked shirt, trousers and brown leather shoes packing under shirt round the left side also a left hander want me to follow in?

ME: No. Don't blow your cover.

Showing hand signs to the guys, watch two men, door, packing is all that was needed. Maddox getting up and going behind the bar with Donavan letting the waitresses have a break in the back and told not to come out till instructed. Topez was round the opposite to our booth eyeing the door and I sat with Jameson shooting the breeze when the door opened and the targets came in.

NIBBLES: In position boss. Crystal has eyes on the girls and they're fine. No one standing out.

ME: Change to earpieces.

I instruct my team.

"Evening gents. What can I get for you?" Donavan asks,

"Two Scotches please, single malt."

Pretty apt considering its Jameson's bar.

"No problem." Pushing a glass under the optic, Donavan asks.

"You new to these parts or just shooting through? If you're staying a while there's some beautiful spots to see. I can recommend a place to stay too?"

"No thanks just the drinks."

"There you go £10.00 please."

Leaving the money on the bar they go and sit at a table in clear view of Jameson and myself right next to Topaz. If he wants an eyeful that's good for me. They can sit and talk all night Topez is picking up all the conversation and we can all hear through the earpieces. Unfortunately, Donavan and Maddox behind the bar can't hear a thing and rely on us to keep them in the know but Jameson, being in secret training with us also has a piece in. He won't be a fully fledge agent it's just whilst things with Lenny are heating up.

"We will hang tight a while, she may come in here. It is one of her favourite watering holes. The boss mentioned we may even bump into a friend of hers and she may lead us to her. We can then report to the boss and wait in the wings to take her out." Blondie whispers.

Looking at their phones at the picture Topez seeing who they were looking at, took a quick picture of his own from their screen and sent it over to mine. It was a picture of Lenny and Gina when they were younger. Well you will never find Gina, she left the area a few years ago.

Scar face huffing "Fine, but next time I order the drinks, you know I fucking hate whiskey!"

"Look, now isn't the time to have a hissy fit and spit your dummy out over a drink, just keep a look out will you."

They hung around another hour and left when Donavan rang the bell for closing. They let the waitresses leave early so they were out of any harm's way and Maddox went round and cleared the last few tables and cleaned up where Scar face and Blondie were sitting.

"Sorry guys, closing time I am afraid."

"No problem. You having some kind of lock in because they don't seem to be leaving?" Scarface pipes up,

"No, they co own the place so they stick around till closing." Standing feet apart and arms crossed over his chest. Maddox showing he isn't taking no crap off anyone.

"Ah I see. Do you happen to know if there are any animal shelters in the area. I am looking for a dog for the wife. I promised her I would the kids one and thought I would rescue one instead of paying through the nose for one you know what I mean mate?" butts in Blondie,

Maddox, standing fierce. "Not around here. Three towns over have one though, try there."

"Great, Thanks for your help." Drinks the remaining dregs of his drink he stood up followed by Scarface "See you again," tilted his head and left.

Chapter 12.

Lennox.

Lazing around all day has been hard work and made me very hungry. Wearing a long flowing maxi dress to help keep my body cool after the heat from today, I swear I thought I was back in South America round that pool. I even have a little tanning going on. Blow drying my hair, how I longed to keep it up but having my scars on show, well, I just can't be arsed with the lines of questioning, so down it stays. Curling the ends to give it a little bounce and touched up my makeup. I slipped my feet into in to my most beautiful red heels. I looked a knockout. Smokey eyes, soft red lipstick on my full lips. A shame I am dressed to kill and no one to see it but that's fine with me. Meeting Caitlin in the suites front room.

"About time lady, come on already. STARVING HERE!" Laughing at herself bouncing from one foot to the other. We picked up our bags and headed down to our reservation. Caitlin wearing a wide legged blue jumpsuit that had an off the shoulder fitted upper half looked stunning, showing off all her curves we entered the restaurant which was starting to really fill up. A lot of these people , who live on lettuce and cucumber are in for a real treat tonight. There will be none of that green shite on our table unless it's a side salad. We were shown to our table and left us a few moments to look over the food and wine menus. After ten minutes our waitress comes over and reads off the specials of the evening with a decanter of water, filling our classes as she recites the menu. We decide on the soup of the day, both medium rare steaks and a good old favourite Eton Mess. Orders placed, I knew this conversation would eventually head to Spencer and myself.

"So... Spencer." Caitlin opened with,

"Yes. He's your brother. What about him?" smiling back at her,

"Have you sat down and talked to him yet?"

"About what?" I replied.

"Well, now that your back and he is baaaaack..." weighing her hands up and down in front of her grinning. Laughing at her expression.

"Yes we are. HOWEVER, too much has happened, too much time has gone past. I can't go back. I need to go forwards and he isn't in my forwards he is still past and staying there."

"You know he is going to make a play for you don't you?" Questioning look attached.

"Nope. We are neighbours and family friends, well more like frenemies if I honest." giggling at her "and THAT IS ALL!"

Not letting it go too easy she carries on.

"All I am saying is this little gargoyle charade game your both playing will end up in the bedroom. You mark my words that this little game has foreplay written all over it." Laughing at her and the people around us.

"Well that turned a few heads but no chance. It has been a while I won't lie and I would like to scratch an itch but he would only knock me back again, why would I put myself through that? Nope. Better off this way at least it keeps it simple."

As we make our way through our meals the more wine we consume the louder and giggly we become and tongues became looser.

"Has Spencer ever talked about me?" I ask,

"A few times he seemed to know things about you that..." Stopping mid sentence.

"Knew what Caitlin?"

"Nothing. It doesn't matter."

"Yes it does. He seemed to know what?" Becoming very flustered, I tap my fingers on my legs a habit I have never been able to give up.

"Don't do that Lenny. Don't start stressing, you know you tap when you do that. All I was going to say was that he seemed to know more about you at times than we did but that was more to do with Jameson than anything else."

"I haven't had any contact with Spencer for years so how would he know anything?" Asking anxiously.

"Like I said. Probably from Jameson as you know the boys are as thick as thieves."

Putting the conversation to one side we carried on supping the wine, well draining bottles like it was going out of fashion, we sat and talked about old times when we were kids and things we used to get up to and how life changed over the years, skirting over my time. Before we knew it, it was near midnight and we were zigzagging our way to our suite. Laughing uncontrollably, we needed to stop every few yard to cross our legs to save us from peeing. I think visiting the facilities should have been a priority in hindsight but where's the fun in that right? Finally making it to our suite the krypton factor of opening the door. Did someone change the lock situation before we came back? Tapping it one way, nothing, tapping another way, nothing,

"Give me a go," Caitlin slurs, she taps it one way taps it again, nothing. Finally, remembering you place the card in the slot not tapping near it we pile in, falling over each other through door as it swung itself open as we leaned against it.

"SHIT!"

We scream in unison as we fall very ungracefully into the room. My dress over my tits and face exposing to EVERYONE in the corridor as Caitlin's trouser legs were up her waist with her top down exposing both her ladies. Good job she had nipple tape on. Wrapped round each other laid out on the floor with one of my legs under her head and her hands touching up my girls, too late for the bathroom both pee laid out on the deck uncontrollable laughter. We eventually unwrap ourselves we crawled on our hands and knees to our on suite and attempted to clean up after finishing whatever was left to pee in the toilet I put on my robe wished my wine guzzling friend a goodnight and fall on the bed. Reminiscing of old times never helped to forget Spencer. His pure and perfect face with a body to match. I felt how hard he was in the ring. Size of his cock? YES PLEASE CAN I MOUNT IT? Thinking of how his lips felt on mine after all of these years, the passion I felt made me do the most stupidest thing to date. I pick up my phone.

ME: Gethout of my hed, I done twant you init!

DICKWADD: Have we had a little too much drinkipops baby? :)

ME: I amnot yuor bayby dikkworld, juts getout my head :P

DICKWADD: I didn't put myself in there Nice to know your thinking of me though :)

ME: YESSSSSSSSS yuo didd wiht you hotips an mucsly body hate you

DICKWADD: Anytime you want my body babes, it's all your :D

ME: Im honry

DICKWADD: Have you had wine?

ME: MAybee whhy?

DICKWADD: It always makes you horny. Where are you and I will help you with your horny problem?

ME: Nott telln u anythin, but youu donet have to be herrre too help wiht it.

And with that my phone rang and it was my frenemy,

" Really baby? How can I help you if I am here at home and you are there, wherever there is? Love your drunk messages by the way, It's a good job I can speak wine!"

" Caitlin. I am with Caitlin."

"Lucky Caitlin and how is my dear sister?"

"Hang on I will ask her."

"Caitlin, How are you Spencer wants to know?" Shouting after her,

"Pissed, Goodnight and fuck already!"

" She said she is fine."

"No. She said I needed to help you with your horny problem."

I can hear the smile from him without needing to see it.

"Missed you Spencer. You destroyed me but I have missed you."

" I missed you too. I am..."

Cutting him off mid sentence, "DO NOT say you are sorry. It means nothing." Hiccup. "I thought we would be together forever." Hiccup . "I really need to scratch an itch." Hiccup.

" Lenny, I"

Darkness consuming me as I fall sleep.

Hearing a phone ring, I open an eye slowly. Shit. Someone turn off the lights it too bright, I place the pillow over my head to stop my going blind.

The phone ringing still, I hunt for the receiver with a hand grabbing whatever it could on the night stand. Finally finding the receiver I pick it and mumble "Whaaaaaaat? Hello? Hello? Hello? Hello?" Remembering the pillow is in my way.

"Good morning. This is your seven am wake up call. Can I offer any other service?"

"Yes. Coffee. Lots of coffee!"

"As you wish, coffee will be right with you. Would you like anything else to go with your refreshments?"

"Any food please like all of it. No papers lots of coffee, as much coffee you can find"

Putting the phone down I drag my arse out of bed and head to the bathroom well stumble more than walk. Crawling is a more accurate description. I realise I still had on the clothes from last night. "Well you minger," as I looked at my reflection. "Peed yourself and couldn't change your clothes," shaking my head to myself I left the bathroom and knocked up Caitlin.

"What time is it?" she cries,

"It's seven 0 Clock."

"In the evening?"

"No, morning."

"Why are you waking me up now?"

"Because your morning wake up came in at seven. Why did you want a seven am wakeup call? Are you trying to kill me?"

"I didn't ask for a wakeup call!" looking at me questionably through one eye, "Did you?"

"No I didn't. I assumed it was you."

"THE BASTARD! I am going to kill him!"

"Kill who?"

"Spencer. The fucking Dickwadd. OHHH He is going to pay for this one!"

"NOOOOO!!!!!! You sure?" With a smile on her face. She ain't to mad now is she!

"Ah this is going to cost him and cost him DEARLY!"

"Can I go back to sleep now?" Caitlin moans,

"NOPE. Your shit head brother is living his last days. I am up your up. You can be pissed at him too and besides breakfast and lots of coffee are on route." As if by magic there is a gentle knock at the door, I sniff up hard. "AHHHH COFFEE." smiling I open the door and let the coffee bringing God into the room.

Both sitting round the table Caitlin asks,

"How much did we drink last night?" Handing me a coffee,

"Thank you. By the way we are feeling and the jack hammer going off in my head. The bar dry."

"What is your jack hammer playing?"

"Paramour!" I laugh then instantly hold my head and regret it. "Ouch." We say together.

Chapter 13.

Lennox.

After lots of wake up coffee and a shower, Caitlin and I started to feel half human again and would like nothing more than plan Dickwadds demise but retail therapy was waiting for us. Hitting the mall was just what the hangover doctor recommended. Not only was Caitlin a world known fashion designer in her own right and designer for the stars, she was also world's greatest shopper. She had her own private line and her own outlet shopping mall with only her designs being sold in her establishments. She maybe the world's number one sweetheart but she never gloats and is still the old Caitlin I grew up with and still very grounded. She has worked damn hard to reach the heights she has. It wasn't a given and still had to go through college, university, apprenticeship, business school and many more avenues to reach where she is today. That being said, she still loves her bargain hunt and always supports smaller businesses, which is why today we are hitting the mall. Caitlin likes to buy things that she can use in her own stores so when people comment on them she can point them in the direction of the little stores, helping keep them in business too and giving back to the shop community. Falcons, her own brand shop, sits on a massive quarter acre plot, own high rise car park for the rich and famous and a lower section for passing trade. People don't see the fierce side to her often, her trusted staff run her stores impeccably and if any sign of trouble or people above their stations. Well, they're out. No second chances. No over ruling just gone. She runs a tight ship but a fun one when you see the real Caitlin.

We study new shops and outlets that have opened and the new competition. We rummage through the old bric-a-brac stores. Caitlin sees the value in everything and has an eye I certainly don't have. She may design the most beautifully, stunning gowns that feel like a second skin when on your body, however, she also makes the cheapest looking thing into major eye popping crafts. Many famous clientele come to Caitlin for one off designs of gowns and suits and yet she is able to make a black bag look real good. So it wasn't a surprise when we finally sit down in a very busy and lively cafe when she gets a call from her mum with a 'Save the Day' chat. Their wedding anniversary is coming up soon and as I should have guessed. Hero themed.

"Hey Gwen, What's occurring?" Caitlin answers,

"Afternoon Stacey, I need you to save a date,"

"Tidy,"

"Wedding anniversary is coming up."

"Themed?"

"Obviously darling... Super Hero's 3 weeks a Saturday with a weekend bender."

Laughing so much my ribs hurt.

"Is that Nessa I hear?"

"It is Gwen, How's tricks?"

"Tidy. Pick your out fits ladies, I only want one of each Hero. I want no copies so get in quick."

I was first off the bat, "I call cat woman," shouting it a liiiiitle too loudly with excitement.

"I call Bat Girl." Caitlin was quick to shout too, both laughing so much we cry. Ending the call we order doughnuts to go. Sat waiting for the doughnuts not really paying attention to the commotion outside with all the hustle and bustle out there. I feel it's time to leave.

It was passed eleven by the time Caitlin dropped me back off, heading to the door I felt him before I even heard his voice.

"What?" I say as I drop the bags and unlock the door.

"Is that anyway to greet your worried neighbour? Where have you been?"

Smiling at him shaking my head,

"Not talking eh? Where have you been Lenny?"

Now giggling a little I can't believe he thinks he has the right to ask anything never mind where I have been.

"LENNY... WHERE HAVE YOU BEEN?" As I turn back to the door he grabs my arm and spins me round placing his hands either side of my head. I am feeling for the door handle.

"I asked you a question. Where have you been?" Moving my lips closer to his I whisper,

"None of your damn business!" I open the door slide in and slam it right in his face.

Un coding the alarm I stand there forehead on the door.

"SHIT!" I say aloud remembering my mistake and opening back up the door.

"Looking for these?" As the smug bastard holds up my bags, grabbing them quickly I boot the door back shut whilst hearing him laughing as he walks away.

Chapter 14.

Spencer.

How can they both lose or turn off their phones. How fucking stupid can women be. How irresponsible of them. We lost contact with them when in the cafe. Caitlin had a call from our ma and then nothing. A good job I had a tail on them. Jack and Nibble were a good distance behind the man following them but close enough to take him down if he made a move. He had followed them to every shop but not too careless to make himself known. By chance, Crystal saw the tail as they left to Spa resort and had the guys on them straight away. Arsehole one never saw our own detail on him. First mistake, you always check surroundings for anyone who may be followed. Sat in the cafe he had them in full sight even with the heavy traffic of shoppers he still had direct line to them. He made a move to take whatever he was reaching for out of his left trainer when Jack and Nibble hauled arse, wrestled him to the ground handcuffed him and had him out of there in seconds.

ME: Situation Jack?

JACK: Ten yards behind target. Blue jeans, blue trainers metal toes, new builders regs, green t-shirt and cap. Parcels are in Simply clothes. Eyes on all three.

ME: Crystal?

CRYSTAL: Five yards behind back up, loose beige trousers, blue striped cotton shirt, tanned skinned, wonder where he has been holidaying? Gucci shades.

JACK: Two little Duracell's heading for a boost. Sheila's cafe, target getting closer and picking up pace. Looks like he is going to try and take out before entry. He has taken off his T-Shirt to confuse the audience, not happening. Plenty of traffic to hide a pump and go.

CRYSTAL: Backups given sent order, this must be him, permission to take him out boss?

ME: Hang tight Crystal it won't be him. He won't expose himself as there's too many witnesses. Wait for my say so and then tag him.

CRYSTAL: On your say boss.

JACK: Nibble and I are going in, he is making his move boss.

JACK: Parcel bagged and tagged.

Crystal followed spare key as he turned around and tried to lease were she pulled her speciality. "Oops, I am ever so sorry. I have just sprayed you with my water when I wasn't looking where I was going. I am so sorry." Wiping his neck with her hand and then his shoulder rubbing it in real good.

"It's fine. Please stop touching me." As he stormed off.

"No need to be rude, I did apologise!" shouted Crustal turning away smiling.

CRYSTAL: Parcel tagged and locked on. Should be up and running Boss.

She is a diamond. Location spray stays on a good week or more, even with a good scrub traces stay around a while. No aroma or itchiness, dries in seconds, lasts for weeks.

ME: Well done Crystal. All fully activated and in running. Stay on the batteries Diamond is on route.

The girls saw nothing but a little scuffle and they left, none the wiser. If only they had their phones on or even charged would have made things so much simpler instead of having to try and follow them in crowds. Even after they had taken out the threat the guys back up would have been around the area, in fact, he was sitting 10 ft away from Crystal who was ready to take him out if needed but landed the bump and spray and hopefully it leads us to the rest of the gang. They intercepted him in time and got him out of there. Now safely in our quarters being interrogated by Jack and Nibble before we hand him over to MI5 as we need to know what business they want with Lenny. Thank fuck for camera systems that we can hack into to keep an eye on them after that since their phone trackers weren't in operation and our ear pieces. like I said irresponsible. There's only one thing for it. I need to take her the vets and get her fucking chipped. I know she sensed me before I even opened my mouth to speak.

"What?" She says, as she drops her bags and unlocks the door.

"Is that anyway to greet your worried neighbour? Where have you been?" I ask.

Smiling at me and shaking her head, Ohhh she thinks she is something.

"Not talking eh? Where have you been Lenny?"

Now giggling at me, she is close to an arse smacking,

"LENNY... WHERE HAVE YOU BEEN?" She turns back to the door ignoring me. Oh game on. I grab her arm and spins her round to face me placing my hands either side of her head blocking her in.

"I asked you a question. Where have you been?" Feeling her lips so close to mine was intoxicating as she moves in closer. I was just about to make my move.

"None of your damn business!" Then opened the door and slammed it right in my face. Game on sweetheart. Just as I was about to bust down the door I see her mistake. She left her bags on the ground. Oh Dear! I pick them up One, two, three, she opens the door.

"Looking for these?" Grinning at her. She quickly ripped them out of my hands and slammed the door again. Poor door. The innocent one in all of this. As I walk away laughing relieved she is home safe but still pissed that she managed to get under my skin again today. All I wanted was to bend her over and smack her arse raw so she knew just how she made me feel. I need this shit show over with so I can find our happy ever after. Just hope AFTER all of this she wants me for her ever after.

Laying on my bed watching the heat source of her body on the laptop connected to her sensors, it seems to be becoming more prominent. "Well someone's excited," I say to myself. Watching her legs move up and down whilst her body is moving in tandem with the rest of her. I see her arm lifting and hold onto the head board. Realising Lenny must be pleasuring herself, what I could only hope was images of me, before I know what I am doing I take my rock hard cock out of my boxers and discard them to the floor just for some relief. I grab hold of my 'pining my for Lenny cock' with a firm grip and start pumping up and down to her own moving heat source. Mimicking her hand on the head board I put mine there too and watch how she uses her toy for getting off. Just as I set a rhythm she changes position and goes on her knees. Riding her toy to help penetration go deeper it seems. I hope it's a toy as I see no other heat source than the lord. I thrust up to her down, she is killing me. Fuck me she changes again. Not wanting to make myself sore I find some lotion and apply. God feels good. Watching Lenny move again standing over the bed, one hand on the mattress one hand with her toy pounding in and out. I hop off the bed in the same position imagining myself pounding her from behind going deeper and deeper hitting her g spot every time. My hand going faster and faster as do hers, mimicking each other's thrusts. I stroke harder and harder as I picture her turning onto her knees and putting me in her mouth I grip her hair and thrust to the back of her throat and I cum hard. I imagine her taking and swallowing every drop and then realising when I open my eyes she isn't there. I see my climax on the wooden floor. When I finally have the use of my legs again I stand up and clean away the mess. I fall on my bed look at Lenny's heat source and she is still in her bed no doubt a sleep after our sex session that she didn't know we just had.

Chapter 15.

Interrogation.

Nibble.

In the underground bunker is a steal, reinforced room. Inside has a lonely chair bolted to the floor with ties attached on both the arm rests and front legs. There is one sole light hanging from the ceiling. An eye scanner and keypad on both inside and outside of the room. One wall with a secret two way glass that looks like a steal wall but in fact a window that connects to the interrogation room which records all video and audio from the three cameras situated inside out of eye sight. After letting him stew for a while, Nibble goes in.

"What were you doing in Sands Mall?" Nibble requests.

Silence.

"I will ask again. What were you doing in Sands Mall? Silence.

"Let me rephrase it. Who were you following in Sands Mall today? What were your orders?"

Silence

"We already found your communication devise. It's only a matter of time to download its contents. I guess you didn't know it records every conversation you have!"

"You can't access it!" He mumbles.

"And he speaks. I think you may find we can. You see. You're a little pawn in this game of chess, a liiiiitle piece on the chess board who only sees forwards. You need to see the whole board to win and that's a Queen and unless you bat for the other side you are no were near a Queen. So make it easier on yourself before MI5 get here and tell us what we want to know and for once, be a head of the game!" Taking a deep breath, Nibble continues. "Mind you. There won't be much left of you by the time they reach you." As a click of the door goes and Jack walks in with a trolley full of delicious treats, pliers, wrench, hammer, the syringe taken from him the prisoner earlier. His face is a picture.

"You can't use those on me. I know my rights. My human rights and you cannot use punishment on..."

"Oh dear. I guess you haven't done your homework. See. We aren't local law enforcement. You see MI5, well they work for us. We find by any means of force what we want and leave what is left to them. So like I said. A head of the game."

Jack was moving the equipment around the tray which has him squirming. "Open your mouth!" Jack demands. "Need to see the size is right!" I grab his mouth by his cheeks and force his mouth open. His hands and feet are tied so he can't resist much. Jack taps his teeth with the pliers and placing them back on the tray. He marks the legs where he wants to hit with the hammer and then marks each finger in order of cutting first to last. It's too much for the prisoners crying

"STOP! I will tell you what you want to know. Just don't cut me okay?"

"What do you want to tell us?"

"I was hired to take out a girl called Lennox."

"Why and by whom?" Nibble asks.

"I don't know who. I never met him. All I was told was she knew things she shouldn't and has a memory stick with vital information on that the same person who she saw needs back."

"What kind of information?"

"Buyers, sellers, imports all business information. She doesn't know she has it or if she does doesn't know what it is. It's heavily encrypted. I needed to lift her, take her to a location, leave her there then I would collect my fee."

"What location?"

"I don't know."

"WHAT LOCATION!"

"I DON'T KNOW! There was someone following me to make sure the job was done, then I would be sent a location. Then when I send proof she is there, I would be sent my fee."

"Anything else?" Nibble orders and Jack swings the hammer round in circles very close to his legs.

"Anything ELSE?"

"YES alright! The stick is tagged. It has a tracker installed on it but they lost the signal. Wherever it is, no one can find a read on it. It must be in a lead casing of some sort as it is the only thing that can block it. "

"Who was watching to make sure the job was done? WHO WAS WATCHING YOU?"

"All I know is that I would be watched. If I hazard a guess, someone close to whoever wants it."

Untying his hands and feet, he must have felt a sense of relief. That was until Jack injected him with the syringe contents we took from him. "Goodnight Vienna!" Once MI5 left with him we went into the viewing and recording room where Spencer was watching.

"She must know what's on that stick. If she didn't she wouldn't have taken it." Spencer says.

"I wonder how she managed to get it in the first place? She didn't work for them. She got caught up in it all unintentionally. They know she stumbled into what was going down. How did she manage to possess the information? It doesn't make sense. Not only that, the tracker doesn't work? What made it stop? Even if she destroyed it there would be some trace right. It MUST be in some sort of lead casing like he said. It's the only thing that makes sense. So if he is right then she DOES know what's on it. Bringing me to the next question. Why hasn't she handed it over to any authorities?" Jack thinks out loud.

"We had full access to the house. We didn't find anything that looked remotely like a memory stick. Not that we were looking for one. Do we need to go back in an have another look?" Nibble asks.

"She is still working on the farm sorting it out for her animals next week adding bits here and there, let's all rope ourselves in and see what we can find out over the week. If we come up with nothing, we go to plan B."

"Which is?" Nibble asks.

"No idea. Still working on it. I may force her into having a date with me so your all clear to go in and hunt. Sound good?" Spencer asks.

"Sounds good," Nibble and Jack say in unison.

"On it boss. Lets tool up." with a smile.

"Topez. You are the animal guru. Keep her on it with the animals as she may slip up. Here,. Give her this." As Topez catches the cap. "She won't tie her hair up because of the scar and Summer here is a bitch. This will keep her head cool and hide her neck so somehow get her to wear it. It's why she always works in the shade. It's a Caitlin speciality." Spencer informs him.

"Leave it with me boss."

Chapter 16.

Lennox.

Making my way up to bed I dump my bags on the sofa seat by my window, quickly wash up and hit the hay. Laying there, all I can think about is how hot Dickwadd looked. looking frustrated and worried was an understatement. I find myself melting towards him a little more. This is not good. I tell myself. Feeling the heat, I strip off and before I know it I am caressing my breasts. Thinking my hands are Spencer's and feeling wet already at the thought of Spencer pinning me down and taking what he wants I reach for Bugs. Turning on my rabbit, placing him at my entrance I hold onto the headboard and I pump away hard, in, out, in, out, my legs moving with my body in perfect harmony, thinking of Spencer's cock hitting where I need it to. We match thrust to thrust. It's not enough. I need to move I picture pinning Spencer down and I ride his cock. I am on my knees riding him, taking what I need. Going deeper and deeper with one hand on my breast and the other keeping Bugs there whilst I ride it. It's still not what I crave. I think of him behind me, pummelling in and out with brute force as I stand legs wide holding onto the bed for dear life. "Yes Spencer. harder!" I hear myself say. Pushing Bugs in harder each time I feel myself starting to nip, squeezing my toy every time I push it in. I am reaching my limit and Spencer is taking me over the edge, screaming out his name whilst I reach my ultimate pleasure. I collapse onto the floor trying to find my breath. I reach for the cleaning wipes, I go and clean myself and bugs then place him back in his little place. "Well done Bugs. You never fail me." Blowing it a little kiss whilst I shut the drawer and fall into a blissful sleep and dream about Spencer.

Chapter 17.

Spencer.

Over the following week was a break from the norm and a little fun. Gordon has had another make over with a nose ring from yours truly and a gold tooth (Sticker of course) from Lenny. Two goons are still trawling around. They haven't asked over Lenny yet but seem to be in it for the long haul. They were tailed in every direction. If they make a move or start anything we will be on there. That was until Saturday night. Group night at 'PAP's' Lads have decided it was time to let our hairs down and party. 'PAP's 'Nightclub was the very first one of Jameson's to open. It was a hit from opening and still going strong. Security is at its best on the door. Head counts and ID checks are first and foremost a MUST. Trained up to notice fakes, even the good ones need a special eye. These guys have it. Undercover security inside for drugs are also in situ. As well as drug dog up front. No drugs allowed at all within the establishment. This is why it is the most lively and safest nightclub around. This week, however, it's the whole group. Lenny and I have called a truce. I say a truce; amicable truce let's say. That is until it is broken and I feel this weekend maybe a boundary too far. Let's see how far I can push it. Bring on Saturday.

Sitting out on the veranda I hear Lenny pottering around then all of a sudden bang, bang, bang. Being the caring neighbour I am, basically a nosey twat, I go and investigate where the noise is coming from and what the big deal is. I stand and watch the commotion. Lenny. Leaning over. With a fucking nail gun! Best view ever. She is smashing it. Two sides up to what looks like some sort or coup. Before I can say, "Want any help?" she had them secure and going towards the pile of wood near the side wall when she spots me.

"Feel free to help after you have had a good view of my arse Dickwadd."

"Give me an hour and I will. I haven't stopped perving yet. It's the most interesting view." Giving her a sly wink.

"Arsehole!" Which obviously she didn't mean considering she is trying to hide her smile real hard. Staring at me with those come to bed eyes lashes fluttering.

"Right fine!" Smiling back at her. "Just put those lashes away!" Jumping over the fence. "Where do you want me? Against the wall? On the hay bale???"

"Funny. Real funny, Grab those last two sides for me."

"These side?" As I grab her waist.

"Later if you're a good boy!"

"REALLY?"

"Hell no. Grab the wood and get your arse over here so I can check yours out since that's what you were doing. An eye for an eye Dickwadd." With the smile so wide her eyes light up. Placing the two remaining sides in place Lenny nails them into place securely. We lined up the roof beams and afterwards placed felt over it and weather proofed the coup. Nail gun in full song. We erected two more coups within the large holding area and it was time to eat. Stopping for lunch, I made us some sandwiches and Lenny made fruit and ice cream dessert. Sitting out on her picnic bench we got around to talking about the animals she wanted for the farm. Talked about the animals she worked with in Thailand, especially the elephant sanctuary. She then talked thinly about the rainforest and skipped a few tales. We cracked on with the more building work and she asked about my deployments and why I returned home. Like she did. I also skipped a lot. Temperatures outside were hitting 30 and I desperately needed to take my trousers off having shorts on underneath. I started undoing my cargo pants when she stops working too.

"ERRR What you doing?" she asks.

"Taking off my trousers, its boiling Len,"

"You're not working in your boxers laddio. Who do you think you are a Chippendale?"

"Pardon?. You like my boxers." I say with a wink. I take off the t-Shirt and trousers and stand in my shorts.

"Put your top back on!" She demands.

"NO! It's boiling, will you put some sun cream on my back. I can't reach Wife?" Smirking at her holding out the sun cream bottle.

"WIFE! In your dream Fleetwood."

"Just do it Nike." Throwing her the bottle over I turn and smile to myself. Feeling her hands on me though, BIG MISTAKE, but pure bliss.

"Margaret Thatcher, Margaret Thatcher, Margaret Thatcher." Is all I can keep saying to myself.

"What on earth are you mumbling?"

"Applying the sun cream was a mistake. Your making me hard so I need a distraction."

It worked to a point. Until she decided to put more cream on her hands and slide her hands round to my front and over my chest. Taking deep breaths, I tried to show she wasn't effecting me. It didn't work.

"Lower," I teased her, Just as I was about to grab her hands.

"Your done!" With that she stripped out of her own clothes and FUCK ME that yellow bikini in full view. She did that on purpose.

"My turn!" Turning her back to me.

"So not fair," I replied but so looking forward to this little charade.

"Life's not fair." She added "Now apply!" Smirking as she turns back around.

"How on earth are you going to be able to work in this outfit?" I ask as I cream her shoulders to the base of her back round to her flat toned stomach. Teasing her as I stroke her body but making myself hard again in the process. Big Spenser doesn't know what he is meant to do stay hard or stay soft. He is up and down like Tigger on a pogo stick. She stops my hand and the electricity is off the charts.

"EASY. I am done for the day!" smirking, "I am going to sun bath for a while before I muck out the barns later. When it is has cooled down. You are welcome to join me?"

"Why do I feel this is a trap?" Questioning her motives.

"It isn't. Look. We need to show face with the gang. They can't keep seeing us at loggerheads. We are adults and run with the same crowd. Truce?" She says holding out her hand.

"Truce!" I reply shaking her hand and pulling her in kissing her hard before breaking away. Whispering in her ear.

"It won't last long whilst your wearing this yellow fucking bikini!" I untie the back and walk away leaving her wobbling. I jump back over the fence and into a cold shower.

Chapter 18.

Lennox.

Every day this week, Spencer has been round helping. He even enlisted the help of some of his crew. Topez, is quite a funny character as well as very knowledgeable at knowing what animals need what kind of habitats they need. We talked quite a lot about what would be a good quality asset to buy and what wouldn't. Knowing what animals are going to be on my farm. These being the animals nobody wants, the odd ones that don't fit. The ones that need saving not slaughtering. He was quickly becoming a very good friend, as well as secretly hoping this friendship would piss the hell out of Dickwadd. No such luck!

Thursday came around and Topez pulls me to one side. I was secretly hoping Spencer would see and have a reaction but his back was turned digging up a little foundation area. Damn it!

"It's really hot again today Lennox. You need your hair up and in a hat. I bought you this, Don't look worried. I can tell you don't want people to see the scar across the back of your neck. I am good at reading people and I can tell this is an issue for you. This is a Columbia Schooner. It has the tail at the back to hide your neck but enough to keep your hair in. Please wear it."

Eyes filling up. I cuddle Topez and say thank you. It has never occurred to me to purchase one. This is really good fabric and looks really expensive too.

"Are you sure? It looks really expensive."

"Yes, I bought it for you. We all have things we want to hide Lennox. I just want to help."

"I will look like Andrew and George out of Club Tropicana but I love it. Thank you Topez, that is very thoughtful of you and please call me Lenny."

"I thought you hated that nickname?"

"Naaaaah, I love it, I just don't want Dickwadd knowing I do." With that, I lean over put my hair in the cap, stands back up, make sure the tails in place and crack on.

Topez leaves me to it and walks away. Watching him walk passed Spencer I notice him giving him a wink as he made his way to the drinks cooler. Finding it a little disturbing then realising it's probably their thing, maybe it's my mind running away with itself. Let's face it, it wouldn't be the first time. by Friday the farm was looking in great shape, adding troughs in the barns and building more coups looked amazing and it was finally ready. Thank the Lord for Saturday nights party time at PAPs. The in place to be. Meeting up with gang was just what I needed. NOW the problem was...

"What are you going to wear Lenny?" I say to myself as I look through the wardrobe of many an eye popping outfit.

"THERE YOU ARE! My little beauty." I lay my outfit on the bed and take my sexy sassy arse to the shower. After a quick shower. I applied my moisturising cream then a little after sun, since it looks like I caught a bronzing today. Win, win. Sitting at my dressing table drying my hair.

"I think I will curl you tonight and add a little bounce!" I say to my hair. Applying makeup, Smokey eyes and lip stick to help it all sizzle and pop. I curl my hair and step out of my dressing gown. I stick on my magic panties. The ones that stick above the pubic bone and the top of my buttocks. The magic pants that show no line. No need for a bra as the dress has hidden nipple covers. Praise the Lord for Caitlin and her unbelievable out the box designs. I unzip my red dress, step inside my favourite little number and zip myself back up. Slipping my feet into my gorgeous matching red heels I stand back and look at myself in the mirror. I zip, zap pop.

"Phone the fire brigade to put me out. I am sizzling people!" The dress starts above my breasts, hugs every curve, strapless and body hugging, it stops halfway down my thigh.

"Perfect." Just then my phone pings, telling me Caitlin and the Uber are outside. I grab my clutch and phone, close all the doors, set the alarm and lock the door when outside.

"WOWZER LENNY. Spencer's going to faint!"

"I didn't do it for him but since you brought it up. Here's hoping." Both laughing at the sentiment.

"Let's do this Anni-Frid." I say to Caitlin,

"Let's do this Agnetha."

"To PAPs please driver!"

Chapter 19.

PAPs Nightclub.

Lennox.

Walking into PAPs, I could feel his eyes on me the minute I walked in. There's a section upstairs always roped off for the group of us. It faces the whole club and you can see every inch of it. Upstairs was VIP only. Not only for us but for the rich and famous. Divides are also connecting the booths to the outside which can be two way, which with a flick of a switch can be seen to a view out, however, nobody can see in. Total privacy. Upstairs also has its own bar with designated bar personnel. Walking through the crowds before we make our way upstairs, we stop by the base bar, high five Gino, head bar man and manager. No need for drinks. He has already rang then upper bar with our orders. The man never forgets and are sat at the table before we even reached it. As soon as we sat down we all clinked our glasses together.

"Bottoms up!" I shout, we all down our shots. Jaggerbombs all round. That's me not sleeping much tonight. Another round came before we even put down the old glasses. Ten minutes and two Jaggerbombs, we were hitting the dance floor when a hand stops me.

"Where do you think you're going?" Spencer asks.

"The dance floor! let go of my hand Spencer."

"In the dress! I don't think so. It leaves nothing to the imagination and you shouldn't be wearing it. Anyone could easily see up it if you bend over!"

"That's the plan." I yank my hand back and hit the floor.

"Come on Caitlin, let's hit the floor." With a smile and a wink I lead the way to a group if lads having a good time. Just as we reach them 'Do you love me?' Came blasting out of the speakers. Being the only two girls in our group, makes it harder for anyone to come over and strike up conversations with. One, out of pure fear and two they always feel insecure over our statuses. Looking at Spencer through the high mirror, his face is ready to explode when we spot a group of lads having a good old time on the floor.

"Oh yes. They will do." Caitlin yells to me pointing to the group. We plonk ourselves in the middle of the them. Pair up with the first two good looking ones we see and start grinding a dance out. I get a little closer, move my arms up and behind me as the man holds one of his round my waist and the other round his neck holding my hand. We grind the whole song out making it our business to give them a good time and a little fun. My guy pulls me in even closer. Who am I to resist. I go willingly and we grind out in perfect harmony. This guy can move! Caitlin, enjoying herself just as much as I am, gives me the heads up that Dickwadd is on his way. Timing is everything. We waited till he got right up close to us when we walk off in a total different direction to the ladies. Eat that shit head. In your face! Laughing as we enter the bathroom, taking the piss out of Spencer and joking about the guys. We hang around on the sofas for a while before we head back out. The restrooms have a seating area before you go into the bathroom section. It has dressing table areas, full length mirrors to see yourself in to help fix yourself up. Like I say, a classy place to be. We head back out when I see him on the dance floor with some wench of a woman. He needs glasses on she is way too old for him, even though she does look really elegant. It panged me if I am honest. The pit of my stomach has turned over in knots. Trying not to let him get to me, we head back over to the group we danced with earlier and had a few more buster moves with them then headed back up for a few more drinks. We talked shit for a while drank more cocktails and conversations were flowing.

"How come the guys who work for you didn't come tonight? It would have been nice to show my gratitude and bought them a few drinks. Especially Topez. What a guy he is." I say to Spencer.

"They're busy." He replied.

"What. All of them? Shame I quite like Topez. Seems to know his stuff." The next thing I knew Spencer grabbed my hand and lead me to the dance floor.

"Why the interest in Topez? He isn't your type and he is married."

"So, I only asked after him. Is the marriage solid?" Teasing him and loving the tense feeling he is giving off.

"Don't test me Lenny."

"Well what gives you the right to man handle me. I didn't give you permission that's for fucking sure!" I spit out at him. "I also never said I would dance with you either."

"I aren't asking. I am telling!" He retorts back.

"Fuck you Spence!"

"That's later. Tell me Lenny. Why would you dance like that with him?"

"A harmless dance has your knickers in a twist. Grow up Spence!" Trying to get away but failing miserably. Next thing I knew we were swaying together. Don't know how that happened.

"Not likely. You come out dressed like you're on show, grind any bloke that is in the vicinity and don't mind being groped. He is lucky I didn't take him down." He hits back at me.

"Again Spencer. Grow the fuck up! It was a dance and you needn't talk. Who was just slow dancing himself not too long ago. What's that saying again? Ah yes, what's good for the goose!"

"She's a friend."

"So was he." Pointing to a very scared looking guy. To be honest I would be too. Spencer is an absolute unit. But for me, never scared me in the slightest.

"Don't test me Lenny!"

"Don't test me Lenny!" I say in a squeaky sarcastic voice.

"You have no rights here Spencer. Those rights dissolved years ago." With that I turn and leave him standing there. I head up for my bag before he could reach me and go down the back stairs and through the exit.

"Going somewhere?" Spencer asks from the alleyway.

SHIT! "Yes. home away from you!" I say.

"Not a chance."

Spencer comes right up to my face "EVERY chance darling." Then flings me over his shoulder with one hand and uses the other to keep my dress down so I don't flash everyone my arse the places me in the back of an Uber and tells the driver to go to his house. Cheeky bastard. "Err excuse me. Wrong address what you need is..." "The address is fine Lenny. We live next door to each other and you're not going straight home anyway. You're staying with me."

"I don't fucking think so Dickwadd. You don't own me. I am going home!"

"You're not." he states back at me.

As the Uber pulls up outside he pays the driver. Jumps out picks me up like I weigh nothing and flings me back over his shoulder.

"What is it with you flinging me over your God damn shoulder Spencer?"

"I can put you over my knee if that works for you?"

"No. Shoulder is fine! My feet would be better though so put me down you imbecile!" He unlocks his door. Closes it with his foot eye scans his alarm I mean seriously. WHAT THE ACTUAL FUCK!

"Over kill much!" I say aloud Who the feck does that? He takes the stairs two at a time. With me still over his shoulder! Show off! And then throws me, yes throws me, onto his bed.

"Why do you make everything so complicated?" He asks.

"Pardon? You're the one who brought me here UNDER DURESS I might add!" I shot back at him.

"That dress says it all!"

WHAT!" Not understanding right. Is he calling me easy or something here? "You saying I am so sort of lady of the night? You cheeky bastard!"

"NO. That dress. You knew it would drive me wild. I always loved you in red."

"Get over yourself arse wipe. My life doesn't evolve around making you lose your shit"

"REALLY! Well you could have fooled me. My favourite colour. Type of dress. Need I say more?" glaring at me.

"Well. Only a self-centred egotistical bastard would think that highly of himself so if the name tag fits your toe pal. I guess it was meant for you! I will be sure to ring the Ducky and tell him his lost soul is here! I can always re-use a black bag from earlier to send you back in."

"Very funny Ziva!" Laughing at himself getting the NCIS remark.

"Enough. I am leaving. Get out of my way. I am not doing this dance with you tonight."

"Oh I think the quick step has finished lover, it's time to waltz."

"ONE! Don't call me lover and TWO! NOW you want to stay. Isn't that just perfect! NOW He wants to stay! Well FUCK YOU! I wasn't enough for you stay before so now YOU'RE not enough for me to stay so get out of my way."

"Lenny. Don't!"

"Don't what Spencer? DON'T???? How about DO! You created this Spencer. You fucked off and left me not the other way around remember!" My anger is starting to hit levels even the dead can hear.

"You were 18 years old Lenny. I had a career I wanted to pursue. I didn't want you staying here panicking at every call that came through. Waiting for word and not receiving any for months or years not knowing if I was alive or dead. Can't you see it was for the best. If it's any consolation, my heart broke too." Shaking in front of me, I can feel his anger and torment.

Laughing at him before the tears started. I could feel them building. How dare he. Storming over to him pushing his chest.

"Your heart broke? YOU'RE FUCKING HEART BROKE! You obliterated mine you arsehole!" Going right up to his face. Standing on the edge of the bed whilst hammering my fists into his chest harder and harder with each blow.

"You left me there. In a heap on the gravel. Devastated. I didn't eat for weeks. I barely drank. I locked myself away from everyone. I was more than heartbroken Spencer. I was DEAD inside. Don't you get it. You left me for a career and never gave me a second thought but left me with no life to carry on with. YOU! YOU WERE MY LIFE!" Tears streaming down my cheeks "You didn't even look back. You got into that car and didn't look back. Didn't give a shit about anyone but your god damn self and you stand there and tell me it was for my own good. That I didn't matter enough for you to stay for. Well I hope it was worth it because from where I stand, you lost me on that gravel path. " Leaping off the bed he pulls me back.

"No you don't," he reaches for my face slapping his hands away he reaches for me again I turn away and elbow him to the ribs.

"Shit that hurt." I say to myself, rubbing my elbow, It didn't faze him. I try to leave again he wraps his arms around me and whispers.

"I never left you Lenny. I was with you every minute of every day. I never stopped loving you." I fell to my knees on the floor. A mirror image of ten years ago and cried. He sits in front of me, wraps his legs and arms around me rocks me and stays there till I am all cried out. He looks at me "I am sorry Lenny." and kisses me.

Chapter 20.

Spencer.

Breaking her heart was the last thing I ever intended to do but not knowing just how much damage I did to her was only coming to light now and it is breaking me just as much. Holding her head in my hands I kiss her deeply and turning quickly into passion. Tongues dancing around like they're starving for each others' touches, chasing each other around in circles. Flicking, craving the passion that's over spilling. She grips my shirt so tightly I feel the pull across my back. Lenny. Holding onto me so tight through the sobs and kisses. We stay there for what feels an eternity but long enough in the same breath. The front of my jeans cutting off the circulation due my swelling caused by Lenny turning me on so much I can feel the pulsing and throbbing through the circulation cutting off. As if Lenny notices, she undoes my jeans freeing my hard on and gently squeezes her hand up and down. "Someone's happy to see me again." In a whisper. Lenny crawls off the floor lifts the bottom of her dress up over her thighs straddles her legs around my waist, moves over her underwear, lines herself up again the tip of my throbbing cock and sits herself down in one solid movement. Tensing her insides I feel her squeeze my cock as she adjusts to its size.

I could break granite it's that hard.

Both of us groaning with the movement. Lenny places her feet either side of me and uses them as levers to help her bounce. She bounces herself up and down in complete harmony with my thrust, her arms clung around my neck. I place my hands on either arse cheek and move her harder into me, the more she moans the harder I bring her to me.

"More, Spencer, More. I need you deeper."

I zip down her dress and pull it over her head and fling it across the room. I take her feet and fling them around my neck and lay her down on the rug in front of me. Pin her arms above her head, bend my legs to have me knees either side of her thighs and thrust hard and deep. She takes every thrust pulsating around my cock with everything she has. I feel her getting close chasing her release as I thrust harder and harder. my knees burning from the rug, knowing her back must be as bad but not able to stop. No way is she going the edge yet. "Spencer faster I am there!"

"Not yet you're not!" With that I stop and take her feet from my neck, wrap them around my waist and stand up. Holding her by are arse cheeks

I guide us both thrust for thrust, bring her down hard with every up thrust. I turn and pin her to the wall. I pull out of her hot, wet pussy and lift her up till her legs are round my neck.

"Hands on the ceiling Lenny!" I growl. Knowing she is safely wedged. I place a hand on one of her tits and play with the nipple as my tongue circles round her little ball of nerves at her clitoris, licking and sucking, tasting her sweet nectar with my other hand I play with my cock. Feeling her pulsating around my tongue she is so close I can feel it, grinding herself on my tongue taking what she needs from me, she takes one hand from the ceiling and places it on my head, forcing my head further in and my tongue deeper. Her erotic moans are making my cock release pre cum making my hand glide easier up and down my shaft. Oh I haven't finished torturing her quite yet. Pulling away from my desert, I release her legs from my neck drop her down to my arms and just as I am about to turn her to the bed she moves me away. Spins me round and pushes me to wall. Squatting in front of me She pulls my jeans down to my ankles and I kick them off.

"You're not the only one who has skills to torture!" She takes me into her mouth, so deep, she takes as much as me as she can till she borks and my breath leaves me. She then relaxes her throat and takes me deeper.

"Fuck me!" I cry with my head back placing my hands on either side of her head I guide my cock in and out. Trying not to thrust too much into her mouth. I check the mirror to the side of me, both knowing we can see, I see Lenny twist round giving me full view of herself display. One finger playing with her clitoris another pushing in and out of her pussy matching every thrust exactly the same as her sucking my cock. Jesus, it's enough to break down my resolve. Pulling her off me, I yank her up and kiss her hard. Spin her round place her on all fours on the bed and insert myself again from behind and pulling her hair back I stand on my feet, my hands on both of her thighs and I thrust HARD. I am so deep I feel my cock hitting her spot with every thrust.

"Faster Spencer. Harder. I won't break," I go harder my balls smack off her giving off additional sensation to her clit.

"I said I won't break. Harder Spencer. Harder!" I wrap her hair around my hand and pull her head back, to the point I feel her pulling her head forward. Oh yes, there's the pull, I place my other hand on her shoulder for extra leverage and I fuck her hard. So hard my thigh bones bounce off her arse so hard I feel a bruise. I take my hand from her shoulder and smack her arse as she clenches round my cock.

"YES Spencer. Again!" I smack her again,

"Harder Spencer. If you're going to smack me at least leave your mark!"

Game on! I smack her and I smack her hard. Hand sore I go back to my hand on her shoulder, force her head and shoulders down.

"Now THAT'S my favourite view!" One red arse in the air the angle changed and I go deeper than I thought possible. I thrust harder and harder, faster and faster till I feel her clench around my cock one last time as she reaches her climax and I spill out inside of her with everything I have. As I lay to the side of her taking her with me, we just lay there trying to catch our breaths. Holding her close, our breaths laboured, she moves her arse back into me getting even closer.

"Careful Lenny. I be fucking you again. I haven't gone down yet I am still hard."

"Well, shame to miss out on it really then isn't it?" Moving her arse in little circular movements. That's it. I bring my right foot up to my other knee creating an arch and fling one of Lenny's legs over it. With one hand I start playing with her clit whilst I slowly thrust from behind into her and kissing her neck. Her head goes back and soft little moans coming from her delicious looking lips. She reaches behind her head and places a hand on my face as she tilts her head round and kisses me. Our tongues teasing each other in rhythm with our thrusts and clit play. She comes quickly clenching her walls around my cock.

"I am close Lenny. Where do you want it?"

Going back to a game we played when we were young and stupid and we thought we knew everything about sex and different places to cum on. It's too much for me to wait for an answer. I can feel the sensation rising I pull out spin her on her back and she is facing me tongue out. Sexy grin and a look that screams Right Here! Taking my queue, I hold her head and slap my cock off her tongue till I release my cum all over it as she goes on to sucking my cock dry. Fuck me I have missed this. Adult Spencer and Lenny are just as fun as teenage Spencer and Lenny. I jump off the bed and put the shower on.

"Its past midnight Spencer." With that I feel myself levitating from the bed as Spencer lifts me and drops me into the shower with him. I say a shower, one that has a fancy seat in it and more shower heads known to man. The man has a spa shower. I thought my shower seat was fancy. This is like a sofa. Only him! He sits me down and cleans me gently and then himself. Stops the shower and wraps us both in towels. I am beyond exhausted and falling asleep standing up. He carries me gently back into the room and then UMPH I am flung and dropped onto the bed and twisted out of my towel on route.

"Oh you bastard!" I shout through laughter, Spencer smiling at the view. I swirl the towel round quickly and whip his leg as he pretends to fall on me. We crawl under the covers and surrender to sleep.

Chapter 21.

Lennox.

Waking up with what feels like a lead pipe on me. I turn and see Spencer is still holding me down. Trying to lift his arm was no go. I will need to slide under if I don't want to wake him but I really need to pee so I need to make a break for it. Caterpillar like movements is the only way I can describe getting from underneath this dead weight.

"What do you think you're doing?" Groans Spencer.

"I really need the bathroom but I have a lead pipe over me."

"And you pretending to be a caterpillar is the answer?"

"HAHAHA!!! Move Spencer before the bed becomes a water bed!" Laughing at me he releases his arm and I run for it. After finishing up I stand in the door way just looking at him.

"Like what you see? Why not be a doll and make breakfast?"

I pick up the first thing that came to hand and launch it at his head. BOOM Direct hit.

"You do know that full water bottles hurt more than empty ones don't you?"

FUCK. Only I could throw and empty bluddy bottle!

"Yes. I was making sure my aim was on point. As I pick up a shoe from his closet but I am too late he has me. "Nice try sexy, next time don't dither and shoot the breeze." Kisses my quick. Smacks my arse, that's still red, and walks into the bathroom.

Laughing at the little greeting I throw on a t shirt from sexy Spencer and head down stairs to make us coffee not really knowing what is going to happen next. I can't just carry on like the past didn't happen and he may have a big problem with that. Last night was just an itch to scratch. Let the showdown begin.

"Nice top." Spencer declares as he kisses my neck and sits at the breakfast bar.

"Thanks. Just an old thing I found lying around." Winking at him.

"Careful with the old. I'm not that much older than you." Came his reply.

"Look Spencer about last night. It was."

"Amazing. Full on best sex you have ever had? Can't wait to do it again. All of the above?"

"Weeeeeeeell." sniggering,

"What do you mean WEEEEEEELL wench!" laughing at each other.

"Look. I can't just erase the past Spencer with a night of sex. We both have different lives now and we can't just fall back into old habits. I'm not that little girl anymore."

"Lenny. I know you aren't that little girl anymore but if you think we are walking away from this you are sadly mistaken. I left you once I won't do that again I promise."

"You promised me you would never leave me when I was 14, yet 4 mere years later you did. So don't promise me shit you got that?" Trying to keep my cool and failing.

"Lenny. We were young and I thought I was never going to leave you; don't you get it. I always thought I would be with you forever. I didn't leave you. You may not have seen me each day but I was always close by."

"I can't keep doing this Spencer. It hurts too damn much." As I turn to walk away to collect my things. I turn back to him, run into his arms and kiss him with everything I have.

"I am sorry Spencer. I just can't. Not yet." I pick up my things and leave not letting him see the tears streaming down my face. If he realises that I can put his life in danger I will never forgive myself knowing I put him in the line of fire and him being seriously hurt. I came home to feel safe not to put the people I love in danger.

I open my door turn off the alarm, slide down the door and cry.

Chapter 22.

Spencer.

I fire up the laptop from sleep mode and check the house. All clear is the messages from the team. A little activity around town but nothing that couldn't be handled. I see Lenny entering the house and going to the floor in tears. I can't believe I broke her so bad. I need to fix this. I need to fix this situation and I need to fix US. She isn't the only one who needs saving. I have been lost since the day I left. I only sleep better now knowing she is next door to me. Even that's too far away. For Now.

It's the first Sunday of the month which mean family group dinner. SHIT. Barbara and Geoff's turn this month. How am I going to keep my hands to myself round Barbara's house when Lenny will be right there? She better wear overalls or my mind and cock are going to have trouble staying on the right track. Heading upstairs I quickly take a shower, dress chose a lovely red wine for dinner and head to Barbara's. I ring Caitlin on route.

Caitlin answering on the first ring "Bro, you good?" She asks,

"Yeah all good. You need picking up sis. I am heading over to B and G's now?"

"No, I am good. Already here. Lenny picked me up earlier. We have a few things on today so we are car sharing."

"A few things huh. Like what?"

"Like a crate full of nothing to do with you and a bag full of keep your nose out!" She laughs back at me.

"Well. If your trolley gets stuck give me a shout I will come and save your arses from the stampede."

"See you soon bro." she hangs up and I carry on driving over to B and G's reminiscing over last night's activities. Oh today's going to be hard. I pull over to the hard shoulder. Time to play.

ME: Missing me yet?

WIFE: Sorry. I think you have the wrong number:) Who is this?

ME: It's your husband. What you wearing?

WIFE: I am sorry I don't have a husband. Just a stalker ☐

ME: Same thing Wife. Now. What you wearing?

WIFE: Can't say. You may crash. You better not be drive texting!

ME: No. I have pulled over. What you wearing wife?

WIFE: You REALLY don't want to know. You may not be able to drive. It could become uncomfortable. You know with rug burns and all :P

ME: Tell me. I dare you.

WIFE: Well since you dare me.

WIFE: MULTIMEDIA PICTURE DOWNLOAD. An old lady with stockings round her knees, slippers, shower cap and knee length flower dress.

ME: Wow. Totally turned on right now.

WIFE: That's a shame as I am with a new guy sorry.

My heart skipping a beat and dropping into my stomach. I know Caitlin said they were going out but she can't have met anyone yet. Topez better not be in the picture.

WIFE: MUTLIMEDIA PICTURE DOWNLOAD. An old man with false teeth, wig on wrong on his head, net vest and shorts on with socks up to his knees and sandals completing the look.

ME: Darn he looks good ☐

WIFE: Yeah. Sorry. Snooze you lose.

I restart the car crying with laughter and carry on driving to lunch.

I reach there in record time, pulling up to the gate inputting the numbers and slowly drive to the car ports. I can see everyone is already here besides our younger brother, Jaxon, who is away with curing the world with his medical prowess. I can tell Lenny misses him deeply being a whole ten minutes older than him, she misses pushing him around, I guess I will fill in for him. It's when we have times together like these is when the missing are noticeably not here, as weird as that sounds. An empty space at the table is more noticeable when everyone is round it but he is living his best life and putting to good use his experience. I walk in kiss mam and Babs and hug pap's and Big G. I follow them into the large dining room where the party is already in full flow. No helpers on the weekend. Sunday lunch, everyone helps in, Babs and Ma always make the dinner. You can smell the roasts as soon as you walk in. Beef, lamb and gammon. Always three meats. Oven on full pelt, three steamers going all containing food on all three sections, three different potatoes mash, roasties, boiled. Yorkshire puddings galore. One thing you can always guarantee on these Sunday gatherings, there is always plenty and enough to have four servings each. I will be putting tubs up for the crew, the mothers will see to that too. I pick up a bottle of water, unscrew the top and take a sip as I walk into the room. There she is in all her glory and I spew my drink everywhere. She is stood there, hair in rollers under a shower cap, baggy stockings around her knees, knee length flowery dress and slippers to match. Jameson has lost it and falls back off his chair, grabbing Donavan to help from falling. Didn't happen. Took Donavan with him along with the table cloth. A vase of flowers hitting Maddox mid flight who is just pointing looking lost. Cutlery flying all over and meat knife stabbing the floor in between my feet. Good job lids are on the condiments still, that may have been a colourful disaster. Place mats and empty glasses all piled on top of Jameson. Donny and Caitlin, trying so hard not to cave when Lenny pulls from nowhere a walking stick and shuffles her arse to the table chuntering.

"A good job the teeth didn't fall out!"

That's it I am gone. I can't breathe. Someone give me air. It's too much. I can't stop the tears from falling and my sides are splitting. Only Lenny could spot this coming from a mile away. God I love her. Mam and Babs run in to see what the commotion is all about seeing the boys in a pile on the floor wrapped in the table cloth, Maddox holding the flowers sporting a lump on his forehead and an old lady sitting comfortably at the table placing fake false teeth on the table smiling broadly.

"Oh well played Lennox. Well played." Is all Mam and Babs say and head back into the kitchen clapping. Best Sunday ever.

After cleaning up all the mess and resetting the table the afternoon passed fairly quickly and game time was imminent. Rubbing my hands together knowing this will get physical. We all pile in to the games den underground. It can get loud, just as Bab's was bringing down the large projector and sets up 'Just Dance.'

"Bring it on." Caitlin shouts. I knew what was coming. She can't help herself. Grease. After a few removals of furniture to make the space large enough for us all the girls nab Donny pretty darn quick. That lad can MOVE.

"Wooooooo. No way. Boys V girls remember. Don't be letting the hair fool you he is still very much all man!" I claim

"And you know ??????" Comes Lenny's quick reply.

"We showered together this morning." I say with a wink and everyone laughs.

"No. We are a man down and you know it!" Caitlin remarks followed quickly by Babs'.

"Now now children all's fair in love and war. You that insecure of your dancing ability and moves Spencer that you need help? Do you? Do you? Do you?"

Ohhh she is good. "Oh dirty Babs. Dirty. Let's have you." laughing at our 'fighting talk.'

"Well. We need to get in the mood for it. Remember the raffle we entered Penelope?"

Barb asks my mother,

"Yes. You didn't win did you?"

"Oh Yes we leave next week for a three week cruise. How Amazing is that? We never win anything. Geoff and I are going on a CRUISE PEOPLE WHOOPWHOOPWHOOP!"

"Oh that is WONDERFUL. Isn't it guys?"

"Yeah. Nice one mam." Lenny and the guys say.

"Any room for a little one?" Lenny asks,

"Yes dear. That's why I am taking your father!" As everyone falls about laughing and Geoff smacks her arse as he walks past.

"But back to the buster moves. Come on, let's dance shall we!" Walking past me clipping the back of my head we stand on our own sides and the music starts to blur out and we start moving. Drinks begin to flow and the party begins. Singing is next, after busting our moves. We decided it was a draw with the girls having Donny the Dancing King. Boys belt out a rendition of 'Bohemian Rhapsody.' We nail it on our knees, arms in the air for Freddie to look down and touch our hands. The girls. Well. The girls go large with Meat loafs 'Paradise by the dashboard light. 'SHIT! Oh do they go for it. They strut their stuff to us. Granny grunt still in her ensemble, shuffling her feet and the walking stick in one hand and vodka in the other up to my face.

"Will you love me forever? Will you never leave me?" As she looks me up and down "Will you take me away? will you make me your wife?" As she turns, bum drops to the floor and back up again and struts away back to the girls. Oh mock me all you want lady. I will remember this granny.

Party time carries onto early hours of the morning.

"I need my bed!" Caitlin slurs.

"Me too girlfriend. Let's go." Lenny mumbles back.

"MAAAA. Caitlin and I are going to bed as soon as we get off the floor."

"Alright dear." Babs replies wobbling over on her pins and attempts to throw a blanket over the girls and stumbles back over to Geoff's knee. Seeing them laid out on the floor wrapped around each other the way they are, they always end up in some tangle both snoring slightly now that the booze has hit. Seven Bottles of wine, that Lenny stayed away from. Interesting! Whiskey, vodka as well as many cocktails consumed over the day and evening. Sunday's are always a good idea. We all refuse to work on the Monday due to hangovers. It has been this way since forever. I sit and watch as Lenny is hugging Caitlin's leg whilst still holding her drink as if it's a pillow and Caitlin holding Lenny's foot as if it is her prize possession. What a sight. 'Perfection.' I say a little too loudly for all to hear. Not that anybody says anything.

Then from nowhere Geoff blurts out.

"Thank you Spencer. For bringing her back to us."

With tears in his eyes he stands Babs and himself up an making his way out the door to bed. I sit and watch her for what seemed an eternity when my own eyes shut down and darkness claims me.

Chapter 23.

Lennox.

Blindfolded "On your knees now!" I am pushed to the ground as ties my hands behind my back and then to my feet.

"Where is it?" he shouts.

"I have no idea what you're talking about!" I shot back. Trying not to let on just how scared I really am.

"Where is it or I will shoot you here and NOW! Now WHERE IS IT?"

I hear the gun click behind my head ready to shoot screaming at me.

"I will ask you one more time. Where is it?"

Commotion going on around me. I hear voices on radios, someone falls right in front of me taking me with them.

"BANG!" A gun goes off and I scream myself out of my sleep. Spencer leaps to my side and just hugs and rocks me in his arms.

"Shhhh your safe Lenny. Your safe. Just a bad dream." He whispers to me and all I can do is cling onto him and cry. I feel myself being carried, laid down onto a bed and cover going over me as darkness comes again.

"What's wrong with my friend Jameson?" Caitlin asks. "Is she alright? That was more than any nightmare. She seems like the old Lenny but different in many ways too."

"She is fine Caitlin. Just fine." Jameson mutters.

"Just stop it alright. Stop lying. She isn't alright and I am asking you now family to family. Friend to friend. What is wrong with my Best Friend?" Pleading with Jameson and getting nowhere.

"Look." Jameson starts, "It's for Lenny to tell you her stories not me. You know more than most is all I can say right now."

"Fine. I will ask her myself and barricade her in till she does because THAT is not just a nightmare! THAT was reliving something. I kept her away for the evening so you could do you're thing but I still have a right to know why!"

"Just don't push her on it alright."

"Fine. I won't. I will stay with her Spencer you can go and rest up."

"No." Babs and Geoff say in unison. "She is our girl we will stay with her."

"I aren't leaving her." Is all I hear Spencer say. Lights out.

Jolting out of my sleep I feel the grip on me tighten. I look to my left and there he is. In all his glory. I lay back down and stroke his face. He is so damn handsome. Then realise I am in bed. Fully clothes but in bed. Weird. I gently kiss his lips trying not to wake him. It's still really dark outside and the room is still and quiet. I can still hear music ringing in my ears and still rather have my buzz on. Gotta love vodka. I sit and stare at him a little longer. So handsome as my hand takes a path of its own down his chest and to his groin. Realising I am fully clothed and he is not besides his boxer shorts and a hard on,. He isn't wearing anything else. Darn this booze, it always makes me horny. Smiling to myself I make my way down the bed under the cover and release his cock from his hiding place. "Hello again." I whisper.

"You're as gorgeous as your owner," As I twirl my tongue around the top. Holding it by the base I lick across the top and then the underside and slowly back to the tip. Gently stroking him up and down following the pattern with my tongue I take him in my mouth matching the torturing pace. Licking the sides of his cock with every up and down motion with my mouth, sucking and licking as I go. I keep it a seductive pace. I release him from my mouth and carry on with my hand as I then go and lick his balls, pressing harder as I move round each one. I feel him squirming underneath me. Oh I love this part. I feel his hand on my head guiding me where he wants me. Following the same rhythm, faster and deeper, he knows me well. My other hand stroking myself racing for my own release when Spencer groans and whispers my name as I climax on my fingers and he pours himself down my throat and I fall straight back to sleep giggling.

Chapter 24.

Spencer.

Chasing after Lenny in the garden when were kids with hose pipes, we were all there but they seemed the fade out and was just Lenny and I. I catch her at the shed and fight to release the hose from each other. That was the first time I kissed my girl. 14 years old. She was turning into a young lady and I didn't like others watching her so I claimed her for myself. I quickly kissed her and told her she was only ever going to be mine and deal with it. The spit ball she is told me I was too late and she had already met the man she was going to spend the rest of her life with and that I needed to deal with that. Unknown to me. I was that man and she made that pretty clear on my 16th birthday when in the house party mam and dad put on for me later that same year. Playing who dares wins and spin the bottle, without Lenny as she wasn't old enough. The look on her face when I had to kiss Mary was heartbreaking. She followed me into the kitchen and pushed me into a cupboard, kissed me as she caught me off guard and whispered.

"You are my forever not hers!" As she calmly walked out of the cupboard. Shocked and full of smiles, I was on cloud nine. Then I was back to the night we first made love. I waited till she was 17. She tried and tried many times to no avail to seduce me. It wasn't working. Until her 17th birthday. We all had the best nights party and later when everyone was in bed I climbed up the outside trestle to her window, thinking it was way more romantic, and tapped on her window. Opening up she was stood there in underwear waiting. As I jumped forward in time to the time she pinned me in the boat shed and dropped to her knees.

"I want to try this!" Is all she said when she released my cock took it into her mouth the feeling of utter bliss. Her tongue nice and warm, seductively taking her time. Twirling her tongue around the top, holding it by the base with one of her hands she licks across the top and then the underside and slowly back up to the tip. Stroking me gently up and down following the pattern with her tongue, she takes me in her mouth matching the torturing pace, licking the sides of his cock with every up and down motion with her mouth, sucking and licking as she go. Bliss. Absolute bliss. I feel the sensation building in my spine my cock is tingling, releasing me from her mouth she carries on stroking me up and down with her hand jackpot she licks my balls, pressing harder as she moves round each one. I can't stop moving. Oh I love the build up. I put my hand on her head and guide her to where I want her, following the same rhythm, faster and deeper, she is so good as I look down at her kneeling on the floor looking up at me I see her other hand stroking myself racing for my own release. Fuck me what a first time. I start to groan the build up is over flowing.

"I am cumming Lenny, where do you want it?"

As I feel her place my cock further down her throat, I whisper her name as I pour myself down her throat and she climaxes on my fingers. I suddenly wake up feeling myself wet and legs like lead as I see the vision before me. Someone must have woken up horny with all the drink she has had.

Normally it is wine that tips her over the edge. I guess vodka works just as much. I put my cock back into my boxers move Lenny back up to the top of the bed and just watch her. My little vixen. As my phone goes off and it is Nibble. "I am on my way." Best dream ever. I kiss her quickly, get dressed and go and wake Jameson.

Chapter 25.

Lennox.

Waking up with Jameson looking at me all worried and in my old bedroom is a head scratcher.

"What's going on and why and I in here?" I ask him,

"You had a nightmare sis. Spencer brought you to bed."

"Shit. Bad?" I reply,

"I have seen you have worse. What was it same one on repeat?"

"No idea. Probably. Had the same occurring one a few times since being back. Maybe coming back wasn't a good idea after all." I whisper looking at him.

"Don't say that. Best decision you have ever made coming back. Talk me through it sis what is the dream your having?" Jameson pleads,

"The same as usual. Tied, commotion, shot."

"Still no idea of the voices or what they wanted?" he asks,

"No. I helped find illegal trade, by ACCIDENT. I just don't know what they are searching for."

"Want to try hypnosis?" laughing at him shaking his head at me.

"No I am fine. I still find it strange waking up there and you were sat next to my bed. Just like now. Bizarre. How you knew."

"Always will be sis. You know what? Come on. Get up, breakfast is ready. We will pick this back up later." kissing me on my head he leaves me to sort myself out. Good job I remembered to bring other clothes, can't be an old woman all the time, laughing at myself.

Heading downstairs I hear the chatter, I walk in and take my place next to Caitlin and Jammy. No Spencer. Strange.

"Where's the unit this morning?" I throw out there laughing at my own joke.

"He had work to do. He got a call and headed out early."

"Oh." I say with a little pang of disappointment hitting my stomach. I had food and took part in light conversation and then made my excuses to leave and go home as I was waiting on animal deliveries today. After dropping off Caitlin I headed home stopping just beside Gordon.

"Oh you are going to look so pretty today Gordo." As I place the flowery dress over his head and zip it as far as I could. Smiling at his newest addition I drive up to the farm. Delivery would be here just after midday so I let myself in and head to the shower. I turn on the heat sit on the shower tray seat, pull up my legs and cry. Swearing this will be the last time.

Sobbing for the past fifteen minutes I drag my arse out of the shower and get ready for today's instalments. I go through the pens one last time and make sure hay, food and toys are there. Make sure all exits are covered and the gate to the outer field is open ready for the sheep. A little after one and I hear the reverse beeping noise coming from the cattle transporter. jumping from one foot to another and tapping my fingers, I am so excited for my animals' to be here.

"Good afternoon, How was the drive?" I ask. He isn't the guy from the shelter but I do know they have alternative drivers and he has his ID on show. I also received a text message to say his name and when he would be arriving.

"Not bad. Pretty clear roads." he replies,

"Want a hand unloading?"

"If you don't mind that would be great. You don't have all your delivery today. The miniature pigs need to stay a few more days. One has shown symptoms of an infection so they are both being treated and only need a few more days to be totally clear. They don't do well without each other so instead of separating them we chose to keep them together."

"Oh most definitely," I reply "Shall we?"

Opening the first lock gate were the three Pygmy goats, all tri in colour and a unique style, one with one ear, one with one eye and one with a bent leg. They are very eager to run around. They literally bounced out of their holding and made a run for it, laughing at the show in front of us, what a beautiful sight. We moved to the next holding. Three sheep, ewes in fact, Nothing much wrong with these, they were rejected by their mother and then said mother was run over, these have been hand reared. Hopping from their holding to freedom I could hear my girl. Pip. My very own sheepdog. Beaten by her owners till she was rescued she has had some training in work and has came on leaps and bounds. Still work to do with her though. Black sheep dog with a white patch on her neck, left ear and all paws, I unlock her holding and she leaps into my arms. Not much of a tail left after it was ripped off by a machine in her last home. She licks me till I have no dry patch on my face. Totally right decision. She is as broken as me.

"Your new home girl. Your new home." Best decision ever.

Finally the chickens. Five hens and an incubator with a further seven.

"How long have they been incubating for?" I enquire,

"Since yesterday so today is day 1 another 20 to go and should see some births." laughing at his own joke.

Once the transport had left I clicked Pips lead to my waste telling her "Let's get our house gets in shall we?" Eager to help, her backside wagging side to side, we sort out our new friends. We walk around the land so Pip has her bearings and handing her treats each time she felt she did something important. "That's my girl Pip," as she licks me after each treat. We stopped and looked at the view for a few minutes and then turned back to move the sheep. I collect my shepherds hook from the barn and head for the ewes. "Shall we Pip?" as we walk to the ewes.

"Heal." she sits next to me and I unclip her lead. "Good girl." Pointing my hook to the right to prevent the sheep running,

"Walk up." Pip slowly walks towards the sheep,

"Take time." Slowing down Pip is perfect and eager to please and getting on with her job at hand.

"Come - Bye." Pip moves round the sheep going very well at heading the sheep towards the field.

"Lift." Pip goes straight into organising the sheep through the gate."

"That'll do, lie down." as she halts straight away. The sheep speed walk through the gate and into the field. I close the gate up, give Pip another treat, a stroke on her head and a big sloppy kiss.

"Well done my girl. Well done. Let's see what else we can do shall we?" Seeing the sheep in the field makes me happy knowing their lives are now a lot more peaceful. Lots of space for freedom and roaming. Heading back to the yard the goats have made themselves right at home already. However, one seems to be a cracking jumper. He is in next doors garden ALREADY!

"How did you get over there then huh?" Hopping over the wall myself the cheeky monkey jumps back into our own yard. "Ah like that is it!" laughing at him bouncing off to the others. Walking all three into their pen and locking the gate over so they can feed. Pip and I head back to the house. Walking in I turn and see Pip sit on the mat with her head down and shaking.

"Come on girl." Tapping my thigh for her to come in but her head moves further down to the floor.

"Come on girl. It's alright come in." I try again. Gingerly starts to walk in very slowly. Couching down I sit on the kitchen floor patiently waiting for her to reach me. She stops just past the doorway shaking terribly. "Alright girl, alright." I say to her as I lay down on my front and place my chin on my hands so she can see them at all times and I gently talk to her.

"There's no hurt here my girl. No pain. Just love. I will never hurt you my girl." Looking at me she starts to back up out of the doorway and sits back down on the mat. I put my boots back on, stroke Pips head give her a treat and walk around the yard. Pip comes close again and seems happier. Obviously the house is where she associates her pain. It's something to work on.

"Up." I command Pip touching my chest, she leaps right up into my arms.

"Small steps my girl, small steps. I am kind of broken too." We walk over to her own pen when she leaps out of my arms and inside her outside house. I leave the door open so she can come and go as she pleases.

"That's my girl you come in when you're ready." I give her another treat make sure her food and water are accessible and leave her to it.

Walking back to the house I take off my boots and check the incubator and to my surprise Jameson is waiting.

"Come to see the pets" He says with a huge smile on his face.

Chapter 26.

Spencer.

I stand there and watch Jameson looking at Lenny.

"Don't worry Spencer. It was only a nightmare." Jameson says quietly.

"I aren't worried about the nightmares. I am worried I forced her hand in coming home without her knowledge and now worried I brought her back before she was ready. I brought her home to keep her safe. What if she wasn't ready to come back? My first mistake was leaving in the first place. I don't want my second mistake to be me not able to be here and save her again."

"Of course you will. You have your team and you have us. We are in our own back yard. You have reinforced her windows with bullet proof glass before she even came back home. She has no idea they're bluddy bomb proof never mind bullet proof. Everything here is on your terms. We are golden." Jameson tells me.

"I love her Jammy. There's no one else for me. She is it. I know she will come round to the idea eventually." I declare.

"Yeah give her time and she will."

"I thought maybe she had Saturday night after the weeks truce and night out but she basically handed me my balls yesterday morning and cut me off. When this is over Jammy I am coming for her. She isn't getting away again. I want it all with her, house, family marriage ALL OF IT."

"Wow. Never thought I would hear the great Marine say that! Never thought I would see the day. I better my tux measurements in." He says laughing at me as my phone goes.

"Weather report shows cloudy spells,"

"On my way Topez." Looking at Jameson.

"Weathers changing. Keep an eye out and maybe carry an umbrella. It may rain!" Nodding at each other I was at the work station within five minutes.

"Let me have it." I tell them. Topez brings up the big screen and we link in MI5.

"These two have been doing a few drive by watching her every move. They haven't tried to make contact or take her out yet which tells me two things. One, they haven't enough on her yet or two, boss man hasn't gave the order yet. If they're finding their play then they must be nearly set up." Topez states.

"Drago, if that's his real name, must be close by if they're making more of a statement. Crystals spray is still showing in the cabin up top on the border. That's obviously where they're hiding out."

"Want us to go and invite ourselves for tea boss?" Crystal asks,

"Tempting. Not quite yet. Let's gain more Intel on their hide out. Do we have a live feed in?"

"Yes. Jack's still gathering Intel from the feed. Audio is hit and miss but working on it."

"We need that audio," I state.

"They're making waves and I feel that they're going to try something to see what happens when they do. They won't kill her or try and take her out as they don't have what they want yet, however, I feel they're going to do dummy run to check if we have something in play." Topez replies.

"Right. Let's plan for each eventuality, scenario, play and counter attack each plan. We need to reverse their plan to gain ours. If they make any kind attempt we will have a back up. Let's go."

"When are Turner and Sinners back?" Topez asks.

"A week. Maybe two. But they'll be back soon enough."

For a few hours we go through scenario after scenario, time of day, where we can take the fight, who is at what position when my phone goes and its Nibble. On loud speaker Nibble says.

"They're splitting up and another ride. Hope you don't mind boss but I called Jameson to head over to Lennox's Just in case they turned up there."

"No. Good thinking. Heading home now. You tagged the car?"

"All in operation boss and sent you the activation lead."

"Stick to the plan guys." and I quickly leave.

Ringing Nibble from the car.

"What's happening?"

"They both followed the animal transporter and hung around whilst they were dropped off. They then split up after the transport left. Coincidence? I think not."

"Absolutely not. Well done Nibbles."

"You get made?" I ask

"Oh yes, like a beacon light boss."

"Excellent. I am heading home to wash up then make my way over to Lenny's. MI5 are heading over to relieve you guy, when you have all handed over. I feel you lot need a break for the evening and need a deserved stiff drink."

"Anywhere in mind?" Nibbles asks,

"Yes actually. I hear PAP's is a great little place. Full of character. Maybe head there."

"Thanks for that boss." With that we turn off the call and before I leave I check in on the camera feed at Lenny's.

ME: Heading home now. How's things?

Jammy: All good. How's the weather?

ME: Clouding over quickly. I have an umbrella though. You?

Jammy: Yep. See you soon buttercup.

ME: Looking sexy there sweet cheeks how about a little catwalk for your old man?

Jammy: You know it baby.

As Jameson starts strutting his stuff around the kitchen Island I see Lenny leaning over, hands on her knees, howling at the sight before her. Oh good luck at getting out of that one bud. I say to myself. Placing the phone in its holder I head home. Ten minutes later I find myself stopping in front of Gordon.

"How on earth did she manage to get that dress on you Gordo? How becoming." I say out loud. "Oh this will take some thinking through." I put my foot down and park up outside the door. I quickly shower whilst the coffee is making and have a quick sandwich and head over to see the wife sending a quick message to the night shift.

ME: Turning off cameras inside the house and turn on trip switches around the buildings. I am heading over there for the night.

Jack: Done boss.

Placing my phone back in my pocket I hop over the fence and let myself in.

"Honey. I am home,. Your husband has returned."

"Oh I am sorry. You're in the wrong place. The place 'You wish for and not even when hell freezes over' is over the wall. Chop. Chop. Off you go." As she walk past me.

I smack her arse and kiss her neck.

"WIFE. Make tea. Husband hungry. Husband make fire."

"Ah bless. Bear grills left an hour ago. You still feeling inferior of him Spence that you have to play Tarzan?" She retorts, cheeky mare.

"Ha! Ha! Wench."

"What you doing here anyway?" She asks through her smiling face. Loving our interaction as much as I am.

"Come to see the pets and have tea with my wife."

"Will you stop calling me that numb nuts!"

"Nah." I reply, "Why fight the inevitable. You know it's happening!" Laughing at me she clearly says,

"Ah yes I forgot. On the 30th of February in the year of never." Smiling at me,

"Now, Now wife. Kitchen. Food. Go!"

"Get out. Fuck off. Bye!" she quickly replies.

"And that my beautiful people is my queue to leave." Jameson high fives me and kisses Lenny on the cheek and leaves.

I stand there and just take her in.

"So about these pets. Show me the way."

Passing me some doggy treats as we head to the door, she quickly stops, turns and bangs straight in to me. I could have stopped in time but them she wouldn't be touching me as she is. Method in madness.

"Sorry I forgot the whistle." She says as she slowly takes her left hand and moves it around my waist to the table top, picks up the whistle, turns and walks out. Electric currents run through my entire body, She must have felt it too by the colour in her cheeks. Oh she knows what she is doing alright.

"You heading to BOYO's tomorrow to help with more of the refurb?" She casually asks.

"Yeah I am. You?" I quiz,

"Thinking about it. Will nip in a while later in the day once I have sorted the animals out. With a huge smile on her face, my girl has a new lease of life now she has animals in her yard.

"Nice seeing you smile again Lenny. I see what you have done with Gordon too. How you managed to get the dress on him amazes me but don't you worry. I will think of something."

"Looks gorgeous doesn't he. Be hard to beat that designer outfit." She mocks me.

"I aren't too worried. I have a few tricks up my sleeve. A few aces to play. Games not over yet. Wife!" Whispering it into my ear. Sending tingles up and down my spine. I am totally screwed.

"Really. Well! Whilst your plotting your next move Gok, let me introduce you to Pip. Come here girl." As Pip springs to her feet and leaps into her arms.

"Hello girl," I say giving her a treat as Lenny gave me. Pip carefully sniffed it, gently licked it and then took it carefully from my palm. I stroked the top of her head "Good girl Pip."

"These are my pygmy goats. No names for these yet however, this one," Pointing to the smallest out of the three. "Maybe name him Houdini, as he managed to somehow jump the wall and back again when I tried to catch him." laughing at the three of them all fighting for the same patch of food.

"Dually noted. Keep an eye out of Houdini goats."

"And these husband, are my three ewes. Looking very much at home and very happy grazing away."

"Yes. They seem really happy."

"A lovely view don't you think Spence?"

"Oh yes." As she turns and sees me watching her.

"Eyes on the prize Spencer."

"They are," I state and bend down giving her lips a quick kiss and walk off towards the house.

"So. What's for tea?"

"You constantly want food. You should stay with the goats." she laughs as we walk on. "Come on big fella. Let's feed your mush."

"Thanks wife."

"You're welcome husband." She replies putting Pip in her kennel pen and taps my back as we walk off.

"Oh by the way. What you going to the wedding anniversary party dressed as?" I suddenly ask her.

"Why?"

"Oh no reason just thought I would make conversation."

"Bullshit. You're not getting any information out of me Mr. You have to wait and see. It's only a week away. You can hang on for that long surely?" she teases,

"Oh. I think not. You need to tell me I dare say or torture is coming your way."

Laughing uncontrollably at me "You torture me? Ah maaaan, that's the best laugh I have had in ages. What's the punch line or have you gave me it already?"

"Punch line. You will get punch line when I tie you to the bed."

"Whatever pal. You keep dreaming. My lips are sealed."

"We will see. I think I shall have my answer by the end of the evening."

"Like I said Keep dreaming."

"Let the games begin wife."

"WHAT!!! ANOTHER GAME FOR YOU TO LOSE!" Sniggering as she heads off into the kitchen.

Chapter 27.

Lennox.

"Right husband. What would you like to eat?"

"You!" Came his quick reply,

"Nice try. Chicken stir fry?"

"Spot on. Where do you want me?"

"Pregnant and barefoot in my kitchen." laughing "Cut up the peppers hot shot!"

"No problem." Winking at me as he starts chopping the peppers.

I feel his eyes on me every time I move so I turn up the heat and play to his beat. Sliding my body in front of him whilst I pick up a cutting board and slide back past him making sure my arse makes contact to his groin. I then go to the fridge to collect the chicken and make sure I lean right over sticking out my backside for him to have a good view. Why does he make me all hot and bothered the bastard. Hearing him hiss I know I am making an impact, smiling to myself I straighten up and walk to the side bench. "Be careful Lenny!" Is all I get. Not taking the bait. I start chopping the chicken and them start marinating is very seductively, sliding my hands up and down the chicken breasts before I chop them fully taking my sweet time.

"Lenny!" He says through gritted teeth.

Ignoring him I put the pan on the heat and wait for it sizzle. I give Spencer the broccoli, sugar snap peas and carrots to chop whilst I find all the seasonings I need, oh dear, I seemed to have forgotten they're on the top shelf. I guess I will have to stretch up and stick my butt out, smiling to myself I reach for the seasonings.

"Here. I will help with that." As he stands behind me presses his body onto mine, totally feeling his turned on body behind me as he takes the seasonings from the shelf.

"All you needed to do was ask." Grinning at me as I stop breathing for a minute or two. Spencer goes and finds the wine and pours us both a glass. Leaning over in front of him whilst I set the table I can feel his resolve diminish.

"Lenny. I am a man on the edge. Quit it!" he pleads.

"Or HIT IT? Which one hit it or quit it?" I say with a wink. He strides over to me. Brings his lips real close.

"Teas done now sit down before I smack your arse raw!"

"Promises. Promises husband!" As I strut to the table whilst Spencer takes over and dishes out the food. Sitting down opposite each other.

"I am glad your back wife. Are you?" he asks,

"Yes. I think so. Taking time to adjust after being away so long but finding my feet." I tell him eating my food so I don't have to look him in the eyes,

"I am glad your back wife." He declares.

"Will you stop calling me that husband! I am glad your back too. I know we are both dithering around and I am glad we called a truce but I am sure we can be friends and that's all we will be Spencer. You do understand that right?" I ask.

"Really?" He questions.

"Since when is friendship all your after from me after that seductive scene you just played out?" He carries on.

"You know what Lenny. We can dance around this all you want for as long as you want but make peace with the fact that I aren't going anywhere EVER again and I am going to be in your life daily as you are in mine."

"Spencer. I can't afford distractions in my life at the moment. I also can't just brush past the fact you dropped me because it was right for you. Things aren't the same between us. I aren't the same you just don't understand" I plead with him.

"Me either," He throws back.

"Make me understand. You may find I can help with it."

If only he could understand the implications.

"Being without you Lenny has left me hollow can't you see it?" His eye baring into my soul,

"Look," I say stroking his leg with my foot "We keep going round and round the same roundabout. If we are meant to be, like you say we are, then it will pan out. BUT WHAT I AM SAYING IS, I aren't ready to heat the pan. Not yet anyway."

"Could have fooled me Lenny the way you're stroking my leg like that." Winking at me.

"Look. We both have an itch to scratch so why not scratch it?" I ask.

"You don't want me for me BUT you want me for your fuck buddy?" He says through gritted teeth,

"Yes. If you want to?" Maybe I have taken this too far, he don't look too happy. In fact steams ready to blow out of his ears.

"Or not." I quickly reply as I stand up to take our plates to the kitchen. He shoots his chair back, grabs me, flings me over his knee and smacks my arse hard.

"Ow Spencer!" I scream. He smacks me again.

"Fuck buddies!" smack.

"Fuck buddies!" Smack. He slaps my arse again and again and again. I have already dropped my plate on the floor.

"FUCK BUDDIES! You are my wife not my piece of arse and I certainly aren't you're slab of meat!" Smack. Then picks me up and throws me down onto the sofa.

"Where do you get off?"

"Well hoping on your cock but that seems a no go." I say trying to dissolve the argument.

"FUNNY! If I came to you and told you I wanted you as a fuck buddy I dare say the plates would have been launched at my head closely followed by a chopping knife. What makes you think I would be alright with this Lenny?"

"So just to clarify. This is a no? It sounds like a definite No to me" Again humour not cutting it this evening. Man I am out of luck.

"A no! Are you serious right now?" He questions walking over to me. I yank his hand and bring him down on top of me and wrap my legs around him.

"I am sorry if it came out wrong. I feel what is happening between us. I also feel that if I somehow call the shots I can handle it and won't fall deep again. I can't have a serious relationship right now, not with you or anyone. I can't put anyone in danger and I am frightened to let you back in Spencer, don't you see that? I need to self preserve my heart. I can't have you breaking me again. I haven't healed from the last time you destroyed me." Hoping he is taking in all that I am telling him. His hands either side of my face stroking my cheeks with his thumbs.

"Lenny," he says. "I aren't a slab of meat. I HAVE a slab of meat that you know up and personal," wiggling his eye brows, "It's yours anytime you want it. But I want all of you. If that means waiting for you till your ready that's fine but you are not dictating when we dip our toes in." Seeing the look on his face tells me he isn't messing around and that fun Spencer is certainly not here tonight.

"Lenny. I aren't going anywhere. I am here to stay. I have a counter offer." he smiles his megawatt smile my way. Oh this is going to be bad.

"Really. What do you counter offer?" I ask.

"We are finally friends again and that means the world to me So. How about we date and see how it goes?"

"Pardon?" I say looking confused. I want a scratch an itch and he wants to date. "DATE?"

"Yes! Date."

"As in each other?"

"Well I wasn't asking a third party to attend. YES each other."

"You and me? No one else? Just the two of us?"

"Yes Lenny. What's the hold up. You want my meat and I want dates to prove I am what you want, need and hope for."

"Don't push it Spence. Before I agree to anything," I say,

"Yes Lenny what? Don't be pushing it when you're so close to closing the deal of a lifetime." Smiling at me.

"BEFORE I AGREE TO THIS...... I feel I need to sample the goods first." Biting my bottom lip and looking him straight in the eye.

"Do you now?" Laughing whilst taking his top off ohh dreamboat,

"Yeah. I wouldn't want to be disappointed with the goods now do I?"

"I can guarantee you will be 110% fulfilled. As you have sampled the delights more than once this last week."

"Money where your mouth is meat slab."

"Yes your mouth is well versed with my meat slab." He says with a cheeky grin as his mouth crashes down on mine. Stopping the kiss I look at him with questioning eyes.

"What do you mean my mouth and your meat slab. One time the other night doesn't mean I am THAT acquainted."

"Oh I think your forgetting this morning wife."

"This morning?"

"Oh yes!" Is all I get as he kisses me again.

Chapter 28.

Spencer.

Fuck buddies my arse. Still trying to call the shots is she. Kissing her to inches of her losing her faculties she lifts my head away.

"Yes your mouth is well versed with my meat slab." I say grinning at her.

"What do you mean my mouth and your meat slab. One time the other night doesn't mean I am THAT acquainted."

"Oh I think your forgetting this morning wife."

"This morning?"

"Oh yes!" Is all she gets as I kiss her again.

I lift my head again and just take her in.

"As much as I love making out with you on the this comfy sofa, my legs are hanging off the end and I need to see you sprawled out underneath me. I jump up, take her with me, fling her over my shoulder, because it's my thing and caveman is my greatest look, and run up the stairs. I sprawl her across the bed, stand back and just take her in.

"You just going to stand there all night or coming down here with me?"

"Going to stand and watch." She stands on the bed, flings off her clothes and stays there in her underwear.

"You have too many clothes on." She states.

"Nah but you do," I throw back at her. She bites her bottom lip and unties her bra, hangs it to her side with her middle finger and drops it at my feet. She then puts her thumbs either side of her panties, turns around and inching her panties down little by little, she leans right over showing me one hell of a view. She steps out of them and looks at me through her legs.

"I like this angle!" She whispers as she sucks one of her fingers and strokes it across her clit. She stands up tall turns back around to me sits on the bed, knees up and feet parted.

"I also like this angle. Shame we don't have a spreader." That's it, resolve gone, I grab her feet pull her towards me drop to my knees and reacquaint myself with my favourite little pussy and desert. Using the tip of my tongue I tantalisingly twirl it around the bundle of nerves but she wants more contact and tries to force my head deeper. Not today. I hold her wrists down her sides and block her legs with my knees. She can't move, can't squirm NOTHING. She is totally under my control. I carry on tickling her opening with my tongue, gently nibble in her nerves and suck it.

"That's so good." she whimpers, trying to release a hand. Holding her tightly in place, I change up a gear and place my tongue in and out of her pussy in again and out twirling my tongue around then back in, torturing her like this is what I do best. I place one hand with the other releasing one of mine to help her along. I take my hand and insert a finger whilst I hold her clit in my teeth and tickle it with my tongue, she is trying to meet my rhythm but she can't move. I pick up the pace and place two fingers inside taking it up a notch. I feel her tighten around my fingers as she cries out in pleasure. Pressing so hard on my fingers, I keep stroking her sweet spot as she rides the wave of her climax. I release her hands and legs. Strip off the rest of my clothes put a pillow under her head straddle her face whilst she opens her mouth and takes me. I slow the pace so she can adjust to my size and then she starts, twirling her tongue round my cock whilst sucking in perfect harmony. Her arms pinned under my legs, which she can free at anytime but choosing not to, that's my girl. She finds the rhythm and each time I enter her mouth she goes deeper. Fuck me this girl will be end of me. I take out my cock and hold it in my hand and start to play with myself as I move over her head and she licks my balls. I take my other hand and insert two fingers into her wet pussy and we play in sync with each other. She releases her arm from underneath my legs and starts playing with her tits. Erotica one O one. I can feel the build up in my spine and the excitement in my cock, I won't last long. I pull away flip her over smack her arse then pull it back straight onto my cock and thrust myself in one movement as she groans. Placing one hand round the front of her and play with her clit whilst I pound hard I feel her tightening around my cock as she cries out her climax she pulls away from me and goes over to her dressing table, stands a stride and lays face down across it. Did I mention I fucking love this girl? I stride over, widen her stance even more and thrust inside of her and pick up the pace straight away. I smack her arse then grip her thighs as I go a blistering pace and brutal thrust. Lenny is holding on for dear life as she tries to match thrust for thrust I pin her so she can't move, the build up in my spine is immense and I feel I am going to erupt.

"Lenny I going cum. Where do you want it?" I ask she pushes herself up from her table spins drops to her knees suddenly, she places both her hands on my arse cheeks and pushes my cock into her mouth. I release everything I have down her throat as she sucks me to oblivion and then collapse in a heap on top of each other on the floor where we stay for a while.

"So. Where you taking me on our date?" Did I mention I love this girl?

Chapter 29.

Spencer.

Sleeping soundly when something wakes me up. I check the time and its only five so I watch Lenny sleep. She has a little smile on her face. Wonder what she is dreaming of.

"Ahh Spencer," she whispers, guess it's about me. Her legs moving in and out squirming under the cover. So this is what must have woke me up. I peel back the duvet and watch her naked move on the bed. She is totally dreaming about me.

"Yes right there Spencer. Ah yes." She places her hand on her breasts, a leg over me and starts to grind on me. Best sex dream ever.

"Ah Spenny," That's new! Never called me that before.

"Don't make me wait please!" WELL, not very man like of me if I make her wait now is it. As I attempt to crawl between her legs she grabs my straining cock in her hand and starts to play. She moves her leg further up so her entrance is at the tip of my cock and she pushes me on my back as she sits on my hard cock.

"Lenny?" I whisper,

"Lenny?" as I match her thrust for thrust.

"Lenny?" I say a little louder. She kisses me and then opens her eyes and realises she isn't dreaming anymore.

"Morning Lenny. Don't stop whatever you fucking do!" She looks at the scene in front of her wide eyed. I hold onto her thighs and thrust up as hard as I can.

"Lenny I cumming any minute. Don't stop!" With that she jumps off me straddles my face and grinds her sweet pussy on my face. Pulling my hair she grinds herself on my tongue and climaxes within seconds, as she then jumps back down onto my wanting cock and rides me till I chase my own climax. "Where do you want it Lenny, she stays put and bounces hard taking what she can get as I pour myself into her." She drops herself onto my chest.

"What the fuck happened there?" she asks,

"You were having a sex dream about me then decided to act it out. No qualms here." I say with a smile.

"Jesus. Spencer sorry."

"OHHH Don't ever be sorry. Just glad I could help you out in a situation as serious as this one." I smile at her. I grab the duvet with her still laid on my place it over us and drift back off to sleep just as my phone pings.

I pick it up and see a trip line has gone off.

"Want a drink baby?" I say getting up and putting my jeans on. She is already a sleep when I turn and take the stairs two at a time very quietly. I ring Jack.

"Trips gone off. What can you see?"

"Nothing boss hold on. Movement round the east corner. Don't have a visual."

"Where Jack?"

"Out the rear door turn right. Back corner."

"Copy that." I quietly open the door and carefully make my way round the building. I can hear the rustling. I reach down to my ankle for my knife SHIT, rookie mistake heading out without being armed. I look around for something use, I pick up piece of brick I take to the corner when the noise stops. They must of heard me. The sound starts again and it is getting closer. I see a morning shadow crouching behind the wall. I make my move I leap in the air to give a downward foot strike before hitting him with a brick when Houdini, the fucking goat, with its horns stuck in box which is dangling from its head looking at me.

"Fucksake. False alarm Jack. Just the goat got out."

"No worries boss. If anything, he is lucky that foot didn't land." laughing he clicks off the call. I free Houdini from his new hat and put him back in his pen. We may need to make the wall higher at this rate. I head back inside and watch my girl sleep as I get back into bed and watch her.

Finding it hard to sleep I go downstairs and make a fresh pot of coffee, clean up from the nights mess and make breakfast. Armed with pancakes, toast and fruit with fresh orange and coffee. I make my way back upstairs.

"I smell coffee." Lenny mutters as she attempts to open her eyes.

"Yes. You do sleeping beauty. Come on foods up too."

"He also cooks. I am a onto a winner!" sitting up and leaning on the headboard. "Smells delicious."

"Nah that's just me." I joke. I sat down next to her placing the ray on her lap,

"Houdini escaped. Don't worry. I put him back in his pen. I think we may need to heighten his pen walls!"

"I swear he needs a lead attached to him."

Smiling at her "He had the most beautiful hat on his horns. Cardboard is so in this season,"

"Ohhh this coffee is so good. Who'd a thought cardboard being a big hit. I must tell Caits."

"I am a man of many talents."

"Oh I know your talents. Don't think I have forgotten all about your early wake up calls either. That's in the bag for another time."

"Whatever do you mean sleeping beauty?" laughing at her,

"Hmmm. If only you could remember eh? I am sure you will remember one of these days. I feel a refresher is on the horizon and heading your way." Nudging me with her shoulder.

"Look as lovely as this wife. I need to head out, shower and sort a few things. See you at Boyos later?"

"Yeah totally."

"What time you heading there for?"

"Once I have finished up the animals, cleaning out and feeding, probably lunchtime?"

"Sure."

"Look Spence. Can we keep this on the down low for now? Just till we are comfortable it's going somewhere. You alright with that? I need to make sure it's right for us both before we tell people."

"I am all about telling people Lenny. People will know eventually anyway. Especially when I take you on our dates."

"Well. People see us together now and think we are friends again. I don't want to risk anything yet. I aren't ready to put myself out there again. Not yet."

"Lenny,"

"Spencer please."

"Fine. But lying to our family and friends is wrong and you know it. It will come out in the end."

"I know. I just want us on the quiet for now alright?"

"We will play it your way for now but only with a little wiggle room." With that I kiss her forehead and leave.

Chapter 30.

Lennox.

I sit there eating breakfast worrying about what fuck has just happened. I can't have him close or anyone for that matter. I don't need this extra worry wondering if they get hurt because of me. I just can't seem to stop myself wanting him. I can't have it getting out we are couple again as it puts him in the firing line and I can't live with myself if he is hurt worse still killed. This is not going how I planned it. Staying away from him clearly isn't working but maybe keeping him close I can protect him. Somehow. "Shit. What the fuck are you do Lenny. In over your head again I see." Talking to myself walking into the bathroom. I quickly shower and change and go out to see my babies.

"Well good morning sweet girl, UP!" Pip leaps into my arms and licks me like she hasn't saw me in months.

"Okay girl, let's get you fresh water and food shall we." As I walk to the house with Pip I stop by and let the goats out.

"There you are Houdini. I heard all about your hat situation." The three of them jump out virtually on top of each other as Pip tries to round them up.

"You're so funny Pip come on girl." As we reach the house Pip sits on the mat before the threshold and dips her head.

"Come on girl." I say trying to coax her in with soft talking and treats. She walk a little way in then backs out again. I follow her out into the yard where she leaps into my arms.

"Come on girl. Let's try this another way shall we?" I walk back into the house with her on her lead but in my arms.

"Shhhh there girl. You're alright." Stroking her head. Pip buries herself into me shaking constantly.

"That's it girl. You're doing fine. Let's sit on here shall we?" Sitting on sofa that is near the window seat slowly and calmly.

"There we ar. Let's sit here a while. What shall we do today girl. We need to clean out the animals and check they're all present and correct. Then I need to go and see they guys at the night club and help work there.

Spencer will be there. I don't know what I am doing with that one girl. I am trying to stay clear to prevent him getting hurt and I seem to have put him right in the middle of danger if and when it comes around." I carry on talking about anything and nothing to her calming her down. We sit there for about 15 minutes. Her shakes are subsiding a little being more intermitting when I stand up to leave.

"Well done Pip. Let's go back out shall we?" Giving her another stroke and a treat in between my teeth and she carefully retrieves it and first check on the incubator before we head out to do the chores of the day. After a few hours of mucking out, feeding and checking they're all settled. I head for another quick shower and head to Boyo's.

ME: Who is present at ones establishment and do we need food?

JBRO: All of us and hell yes!

ME: On route.

JBRO: See you soon sis.

As soon as I walk in I feel the sensation someone's watching me. I carry on as if I aren't rattled. "Afternoon Cathie. Can I place an order to go?"

"You certainly can my darling. What you needing?"

"Six portions of fish and chips with salt and vinegar on all with four large gravies. Four large peas. Six bread buns and six bottles of water please" I go and sit in my favourite booth and casually look around. No one standing out. I look closely again not being able to shift the feeling.

Knock. Knock. Knock. I jump out of skin when I look at the window and Topez is there waving.

"Shit." I shout out loud as he walks in. "You scared the shit out of me then." I say laughing at him but obviously my face must show an alternative picture than the one I am trying to give.

"Sorry Lenny. You eating in or out?"

"Out. Heading the Boyos with food for the troops."

"I am so sorry I scared you. I didn't intend to I apologise. What's on the offering?"

"Fish and chips all round. What else?" I say laughing. "You?"

" I just nipped for a sandwich nothing flash. Just to tide me over."

"How's Boyos coming along?"

"Alright. I think. I will soon know. It's opening night in a few weeks so need it up and running. I can't wait but need hands on deck so if you're available hint, hint, HINT!" My eyes bulging towards him and with a cheeky grin. laughing at me.

"I wish I could but working on something for the boss man so need to pass I am afraid. But we have finished the security in there and it was taking shape the last time I checked."

"He works you too hard,"

"Orders up Lenny!"

"Thanks Cathie. Was nice bumping into you again. You need to nip round and see the animals. They're not all here yet but sheep and goats are, a few hens and my girl Pip."

I go to the counter and pick up a the bags of food.

"Hang on Lenny I will help you to the car."

"No it's fine you order your sandwich."

"No honestly. I can nip back in for it. Here, let me." As he takes the bags out of my hands and walks me to my car. Placing the food on the backseat I say good bye and start up the car.

"Thanks Topez. See you soon."

"No problem Lenny." As I watch him go back to his car. Strange. He didn't go back in for his sandwich. I head out to Boyos and Topez is behind me as he drives to work or wherever he is off too. I wave bye to him and pull up in Boyo's car park and beep my horn to let them know I have arrived with food and there he is my sex toy running out to great me with a chaste kiss when I say.

"Food. Back seat. Need the bathroom. Gotta go!" As I throw my keys to him and run in Boyos. I run through the door and sit on the floor with the rest of the gang waiting for the food to be brought in.

"Where's the food sis?" Jameson asks,

"Yeah sis, where's the food?" Maddox chips in.

"The hobby horse is bringing it in." I say smiling.

"Needing a bathroom huh?" He says arms full walking in the door.

"Yep," I say laughing, trying to hide my uneasiness from the cafe. Just can't shake off this feeling.

"You two drive me insane." Jameson laughs back.

"Dish the goodness my friend. Dish the goodness. I am starving." As we all sit on the dance floor with the lights going different colours and eat lunch.

Chapter 31

Spencer.

Fixing the last work top into place my phone goes off in my pocket. I take it out and see it's Topez so I put it on speaker and lay it on the work top.

"You're on speaker Topez. What's up?

"Is it safe to talk?"

"I am here Topez." Jameson replies, "Good. I saw Lenny going into Cathie's and she was being watched and followed. I followed her in. She looked a little uneasy and jumpy like she could feel something was off. Anyway I stayed and made chitchat, walked her back to her car and followed her to you. She is pulling up in the car park in a few minutes. They're closing the gap but they saw me going in after her and they left.

They're about two cars behind me. I thought they would have shown their faces in PAP's the other night but they didn't. She is pulling in now."

Beep. Beep. Beep.

"Thanks Topez. I will take it from here. Good work Toe."

"Just my job boss man. I will be in touch. Going off the grid for a few."

"You know what to do. Be careful."

"Check that." I close the call and run outside to Lenny. Looking at Jameson the way.

"A storms brewing."

"Time to batten down the hatches?"

"Could be."

Eating our lunch on the dance floor was bit surreal with the lights flashing round us. It is looking amazing.

"So. What's left on the list to do?" I ask him.

"They're coming tomorrow to finish the pumps and wiring to the kitchen then that's cosmetic and nearly finished. Paint touch ups and titivating the place and we will be there. Just unpacking the tables and chairs. A little finishing off at the band area and DJ box. All in all on target I feel. I had an email from Blackout. They have confirmed and will play the first Four weekends Friday and Saturdays so that's ticked off too."

"Is it strictly ticket opening night?"

"Yes. All sold. Even before we knew who was playing. Everybody wants' a bit of the BOYO's it seems." All laughing at the sentiment.

"Oh good. Live bands, means girl groups. I am all over that." Maddox chips in. "We are having booths aren't we?"

"Yes Maddox of course we are numb nuts!"

"Hey I call Dickwadd that. Find another pet name for him!" Lenny pipes up.

"We will be able to see all the surroundings so you will have a good view I promise."

"Good. None of this settling down shit for us guys. Only young once. Live life to the max is what I say. I have far too much to do in my life before I settle down."

"Yeah like what?" Jameson s asks him,

"LIVING Jameson, Living."

"I live just fine."

"Yeah you keep telling yourself bro. One of these days you might even believe it. Bring on opening night boys. You know what this means don't you... GROUPIES!"

Howling with laughter Lenny pipes up.

"Ah I forgot about the groups and their groupies. So what Blackout like? Men, woman, ages???????"

"Male group. Five of them. Our ages and they're amazing. Caitlin showed me them."

"Caitlin."

"Yeah Lens,"

"Do I know Blackout? Have I heard or seen them?"

"Yeah I am sure you have one time or other." looking very sheepish,

"I will go on you tube and have a gander. You never know I may find me new husband."

"Oh we can be the groupies Lenny. You in?"

"Damn right girlfriend."

"We need a plan Caits. Let's form a plan."

"Sign me up, I AM IN."

"Err. Steady ladies. You know we are here right?"

"Yes. However. Opening night, make sure you are MILES away from us."

And if you think that's happening WIFE your very much mistaken!"

"Blah. Blah. Blah." Is all I get and we carry on working a few hours more.

"Well folks," Lenny declares, "I have animals to feed and bed down for the evening. So I am out of here."

"Me too. Not the animal part. Just a shower as I stink!"

"That's called hard work. It's about time you were introduced to it." Lenny throws out as she leaves.

"I will see you guys later." Laughing as I leave.

I hang around in the doorway a few minutes till she has left and see if anyone follows her. Green pick up again. I hop into my car and follow suit. They must clock me as they pull off towards town. Nibbles is two cars behind me and pulls off to follow the pickup. The spray will be starting to fade off ago soon and I don't think we will get another opportunity to re-cover. Unless there's air con in the farm house that we can feed some through. Highly unlikely but worth looking into. A few scenarios run through my mind on the way home. I see Lenny is safely home and head in to shower.

Once showered I sit and watch a few images of trips on the cameras. Nothing much to be concerned about. Jack would have seen anyway and alerted me so I set about going through a few more scenarios when I heard Lenny screaming "No, No, No, No, GET OFF IT!"

I fly outside to see the craziness unfold. Lenny running around my garden after Houdini, who is out over the wall again, with one of Lenny's bras over his horns. Well I say over his horn. Over one horn and under his chin. I stand and laugh. I then pick my phone up and hit record. THIS is comedy gold.

"Get here NOW Houdini. Here!" Pip is sat on the wall her head leaned to one side taking in the scenes as much as I am but looking really confused.

"So I guess you're not going to help then?" However who that's aimed at is beyond me. is it me? Houdini? Pip? The options are endless.

"Whom would that be addressed too?"

"SHIT." She jumps round to see me.

"You scared the bejeebers out of me arsehole. You could help if you're wanting to?"

"Oh why would I do that? The show is far more exciting with just you and Houdini."

"Ha! Ha! A little help please."

I hop over the wall into the feeding bags and hop bag over. Pip barks a little Well Done to me. I stand there throw some food on the floor. Like dolphins to water Houdini jumped towards me eats the food from the floor and then eats it from my hands. As he does I hold onto his horns free him from the killer bra then pick him up and place him back over the wall.

"THANKYOU." She says all out of breath.

"Your very welcome. I think this maybe yours?" As I hover the bra above my head.

"Hmmm I think so." As she tries to jump up and grab it.

"Spencer. I kind of need the bra."

"Oh no you don't. Your nipples look just fine through you're top." She digs me in the side and I pretend she caught me good. As she tried to take the bra I scoop her and kiss her.

"Thanks for the entertainment. Want a brew? It's the least I can do for payment."

"Words to my ears. Brew up sex toy. I will go and attempt to lock Houdini and his Harem up and be right back with you."

Sitting out on the decking with Lenny laid between my legs was the perfect chance to raise up her jitteriness.

"You seem like you have been rather edgy today. All ok?"

"Yeah why?" As she shifts on the seat.

"You just seemed really edgy. You know you can tell me anything right?"

"Yeah I know. Look I better get going. I need to sort out the pets and stuff you know how it is. I am a regular Dr Doolittle."

"Piss off Dr Doolittle. You certainly did little earlier when you couldn't control your goat," laughing at her.

"Look. I know you Lenny and something is on your mind. What is it?"

"Nothing alright! I am fine. Just leave it."

"Lenny." But she walks away without a backward glance.

I go in and message the boys.

ME: Campfire meeting

Jammy: On way

Donny: I will bring marshmallows

Maddox: I will bring alcohol

Within fifteen minutes the boys are sat around the fire on the decking.

"We need Lenny to tell us what's happening and we need to bring her in on what we are doing."

"Are you mental? She will have our balls in vices." Maddox states,

"Look. Did you see how jumpy she was today. On edge. Even in Boyos. She was just a jumpy earlier. I have a feeling she feels something is up and won't say anything. Jameson, has she mentioned anything to you?"

"No. Not really. Just when she woke up Monday and I was there she still says she doesn't understand how I was there when she woke up in the hospital when the shit storm went down last time. Look we know they're closing in and it's what we want and it is only a matter of time when they make their move. Do we get a head of the game now and let her in on it or feel her wrath when she figures it out herself?"

"For you lot it will be fine. When she knows it's been a game plan from me THAT'S when shit storm Lenny will hit. She will hate me and won't want anything to do with me anymore and we just..."

"Just what?" Donny asks,

"Just got back to being us. She still doesn't trust me and after this I can only agree with her. I promised her I won't be going anywhere ever again.

She may just make me leave after this and then I lose her all over again. However, this time the only consolation will be she will be free and safe."

"So. What's the master plan? We telling her or waiting it out?"

"Look. I will bring her to the bunker house tomorrow and we will all meet there and lay it all out. If she knows in advance something maybe playing out she will be ready. I will be in the dog house but what's new right?"

"Are we telling her how you saved her and everything else?"

"I don't think we need to. Unless it comes up."

"Well. It probably will won't it?" Donny looking worried,

"Look. She is your sister and you do what makes you feel better. ME? I just need her to know I aren't just doing this out of courtesy. I am doing it because I love her guys. Yes. She is my friend too but she is it for me. No more fucking about I just hope she still wants to be with me after this shit show is over."

"Hey," Maddox interrupts,

"You are her always and forever. We know that even she does and if she takes a hissy fit then I will sort her out for you." As everyone laughs at him but loving the sentiments.

"We are in this together and once she realises it's all for her. She will be fine."

"Here's hoping," We all clack bottles and talk about how we are going to approach it. After the boys leave I message Lenny.

ME: Evening wife. You awake?

WIFE: No I am asleep Dickwadd, of course I am awake. Have the guys gone?

ME: Yeah. Fancy some company?

WIFE: I will be right over.

I lay on the sofa and wait for her to come in when the French door slides open and closed. I look up and the vision that's standing before me Lenny in a raincoat, high heels and hiding something behind her back. This is going to be good.

"Didn't know it raining?"

"Yeah goats and bras." I can't help but laugh,

"However, seems dry in here!" As she unwraps her belt opens up the coat an drops it to the floor. There. Standing feet apart, in all her gory, was Lenny in a black suspender belt, fish net stockings that make her legs go for miles in high heels shoes and holding a spreader out in front of her. Instantly hard I have a tent in my shorts.

"Want a play?" Is all she needed to say. I leapt off the couch took her face in my hands and smashed my lips down on to hers. Passion was instant and I was rock hard. She dropped the spreader as I picked her up and she wrapped her legs around my waist.

"Hold on." Is all I say to her as I leave go of her arse and drop down my shorts and press her against the wall as I step out of them.

"I didn't know you were so kinky Wife?"

"Well if I can't dress up and play with my husband. What's the point? Now put your cock in me. Fuck me hard. Make me cum and then do what you like to me!" I bring her down on to my rock hard cock and thrust inside of her. I take her wrists and pin them above her head as I pound in to her. It doesn't take her long before she is squeezing my cock as she comes around it.

"That's one!" I say as I keep hold of her and take her in to the dining room. Sitting her on one of the chairs I tell her to stay. I run in to the kitchen and pick up two tea towels and tie her ankles to the bottom part of the legs of the chair. I then tie her wrists behind the back of the chair with the belt of her coat. I would love to blindfold her but even I know that's pushing a boundary knowing what hell she went through. I stand in front of her.

"Open your mouth Lenny," She does so as I place myself in side her mouth and she gently sucks the top and twirls her tongue around the underside then bit by bit after each suck she takes me deeper. I fling my head back and moan. This feels so good. I can't bare it too long as I will shoot my load far too early. I pull out and take it in my hand and flick her nipple with it then the other one. I carefully sit in between her spread legs. Kiss her. Our tongues dancing with each others as I insert two fingers into her. She is so wet. I stroke her G Stop with my fingers as I play with her clit with the other I can feel her clamping down on my fingers. I take them out and slide my cock in. Sat this way she is so tight. I tilt her up a little by her arse so I fit all the way in and then gently place her back down again. I thrust slowly in and out, so slowly its making her writhe underneath me.

"I need it faster Spencer!"

"Not yet you don't!" As I give her a little more but not much, taking her face in my hands and kiss her passionately I can feel my own climax stirring I pull out and kneel in front of her and let my mouth take her. Coming hard on my tongue within minutes.

"That's two."

"How many we going for?" she asks breathlessly.

"As many as we can baby." Kneeling up I take her nipples between my fingers and roll them. She is trying to catch her breath but I won't let her. I undo her hands and feet stand her up off the chair and sit her on the table. I place her feet either side of her thighs and enter her I pull her head back exposing her neck. Kissing and nibbling away on her as I thrust in and out at a fast pace. So fast, I can't control my movements, they're in total sync with Lenny's as we bounce off each other and match the hits pound for pound. She has hold of me behind my neck with one hand and the other holding her up on the table behind her. I quickly pull out fling her over my shoulder, pick up the spreader as I run up the stairs. I fling her on the bed only attaching her ankles at first to the straps and open her up and slide in to her as we match thrust for thrust.

"I want you to open me wider husband!" I pull out and widen her legs.

"I won't break and very flexible. NOW OPEN ME THE FUCK UP!" she orders me.

"My FUCKING PLEASURE." I spread the bar as far as it will go. Spread in front me at twenty past eight. I take in the vision. She starts to play with one of her breast with one hand and plays her centre with the other and I stand there stroking my cock watching each other pleasure ourselves. I go to the cabinet in the bathroom and come back with some baby oil. I drip it slowly across her breasts. I then kneel either side of her on the bed and place my cock between her breasts as she presses them together and I thrust up and down between them. With the oil my cock glides up and feels so good. Lenny lifts her forward to catch the top of my cock every time and sucks it. The pleasure is immense. I stand up, attach her hands to the straps grab the spreader and fling her over. Arse in the air, shoulders and head on the bed not able to move I straddle her, grip her thighs tightly as she is pinned to the bed and take her from behind. I grip her hair in my hand and see her scar, fury over comes me and I pound so hard her screams of pleasure hit a new high as she comes undone around me.

"That's three," groaning,

"My turn," she cries as I undo the spreader and stand in front of her. She takes it from my hands and places it on the floor behind the front legs of the room chair pushing me to sit she straps my feet in. Not able to move my legs she drops to her knees and takes me in her mouth. I hold her by the head whilst she takes me deep and I match her thrust to suction. She stands, turns, straddles me as she sits down on my cock. Sitting reverse cowgirl and uses her feet for leverage to bounce. She places her hands on her knees and raises her arse up and down giving me the most amazing view seeing her take me in perfect rhythm. Smacking her arse as hard as I can she clenches round me each time I smack her. I grip her hair. Pull her head back and pull her down harder. I can feel my balls tightening and I know I am close. She picks up the pace and I can't help but thrust. "Lenny I am close. Where do you want it?"

She jumps off me spins onto her knees wraps her tits around my cock again and stroke me and I erupt all over her.

"That's four," she cries with a sexy grin.

"Jesus Lenny. You trying to kill me off or what?" I say laughing.

"Fuck me, you're not leaving ever!" As I go to untie my feet with shaking hands she stands in front of me.

"You're not done yet!" puts me to my knees and brings my head to her centre.

"I guess we are going for five!"

Chapter 32.

Spencer.

As I lay there stroking her back and watch her sleep for what feels an eternity, her little puddy nose wrinkling like she is a witch from bewitched. This is going to be one great day or shit day.

"Stop looking at me and bring me coffee husband!"

"Yes your majesty!" As I lean over her and waft it in front of her nose,

"Oh I knew I married you for a reason," smiling she opens her eyes, "That feels nice."

"We are all meeting in the bunk house later and we want you to be there." I blurt out way too fast and looking at me worriedly.

"Why?"

"We just need a bit meet. What had you so rattled yesterday?"

"Nothing had me rattled. Topez scared me a little in Cathie's knocking on the window. Maybe that's what your worried about but I am fine. Everything is fine." Turns her face to the opposite way.

"Lenny. I know when you're hiding something so spill!"

"I am fine Spencer. Nothing going on here!"

"I call bullshit. What's going on Lenny?"

"FINE. Lately I feel like I am being watched. I had a feeling in Cathie's yesterday but nothing was out of the ordinary then Topez knocked on the window and made me jump. That's all."

"Right. So, why would you think someone would be watching you?"

"I don't know. I just can't shake a feeling that's all so end of discussion."

I stroke up to her neck and she clenches, "I don't think so. What's this scar on your neck?" Freezing for a split second,

"There's nothing to talk about it. I caught it on a wire one time its fin. Drop it."

"It's more than wire. Why don't you tell me all about it?"

"Maybe because I don't want to!"

"Did you do it on one of your travels? Why did you come back to Whitesands?" I know I am pushing hard and I shouldn't, my backs up and I want her to trust me.

"None of your damn business Spencer. Drop it. What's with the third degree?"

"Just making conversation Lenny."

Lenny flips me on to my back and pours the baby oil over me. Massaging my back and really getting her elbows right in feels bliss. I know I have pushed too hard as she changes tactics.

"Lower." I tell her. She goes to the legs and stops. I know she sees what I wanted her to.

" Well whilst on the subject of scars. What happened to your leg?" Questioning me.

"I cut it on a wire!"

"Bullshit!" As she traces her fingers over the scars that go across the top back of my leg and downwards like a perfect capital T.

"Yes. I definitely call bullshit! Why did you come back? I am glad you did don't get me wrong but I would like to think you came back because you heard I was. However, I have a deeper feeling it isn't."

"Get over yourself Spencer. I came back because it was time. I didn't even know you were back till the first time we bumped into each other." As she travels her hands back up to my back.

"Why don't you tell me some stories about your travels and you're life after here. I bet you have some amazing ones to tell."

"No. They're none of your business."

"Tell me Lenny."

"Look. I saw animals. I looked after animals I came back and got my own animals end of story now drop it!"

"Look Lenny there's no need to be so angst. I am only making conversation. I thought it would be nice if we got to know each other again. We haven't saw each other for nearly ten years that's a great big chunk of time to cover." I know I am pushing again but I need to see if she will give me at least something.

"NO Spencer enough. I need to go and sort the animals out. What time is everyone meeting at the bunkhouse? I may not be able to make it."

" 11 O Clock and you will make it or I will come and get you myself."

"Whatever. I need to go." Before I could stop her she was up and gone.

ME: Bunkhouse 11 O clock. I think I have already made her pissed so good luck today guys. (thumbs up emoji)

Maddox: Shit. Better wear a cup (Hiding emoji)

Jameson: Oh Dear, and a head guard (boxing glove emoji)

Donny: Glad it's you and not me, and breast guard.

ME: I am going to stand behind Perspex glass :) You lot find your own cover :P

Chapter 33.

Lennox.

Why did he need to push everything we say or do to the limit. I want to forget not constant reminders. How could I tell him. I feel people watching me because I got myself into trouble. Unintentionally, sort of but still trouble. I don't know if I can handle this after all. Maybe I should leave again but what will happen to my little family of animals? I can't leave them now. No. I need to think things through before it all gets out of hand AGAIN.

I am mucking out the animals when I hear a car pulling up.

"Hey Lenny," I hear Caitlin shout with a wave, "I have outfits baby!"

"WHOOHOOOOO I cannot wait to see us in these. Tomorrow has came round so quickly for this party don't you think?"

"My goodness yes. But you know me. Thrive under pressure and we will look like Bells of ball in these costumes. Let's go and try them on!"

We both run inside like teenagers getting ready for our first party.

"Ah YES! Look at us. Cat woman and Batgirl at your service Mr Wayne!" Laughing in unison.

"The guys are going to go ape shit. It's going to be hilarious."

"Spencer will go ape shit when he sees you like that girl WOWZER."

"Nah. He is too busy loving himself for noticing me." I say with a large smile,

"Yeah! Yeah! Yeah! I smell bullshit, especially with that smile." Winking at me.

"Oh I don't know what to do Cait's. I am just not dealing with things like I should be."

"What do you mean?"

"I tried staying mad at him that didn't work. Tried being friendly at arm's length. That didn't work. Tried..."

"What do you mean didn't work?"

"You know the itch we talked about? Well it's been getting scratched."

"I KNEW IT!" Jumping up punching the air in her super hero outfit. I creased over.

"You looked so funny then. A real hero," laughing uncontrollably.

"How on earth did this start?"

"Oh I don't know. We argued. We kissed. We scratched. What can I say?" Holding my hands out.

"So, what does this mean that you are starting things back up properly or what?"

"No. I wanted friends with benefits. Can you believe it. He refused! Refused! What man in his right mind would refuse a no commitment, free sex?"

"HE DID NOT?"

"Yeah he did. He said he wasn't a piece of meat and felt offended."

"So what happened?"

"He came back with a counter offer,"

"A counter offer. You're kidding me right? What man wouldn't want a no ties relationship?"

"You're brother that's who."

"So what does he want in return?"

"Dates!"

"Dates?"

"Yes dates. If I want to scratch and itch he gets a date!"

"EH?" Is all she can say between hysterical laughter.

"Only my brother can con you into a relationship."

"It's not a relationship it's a friends with benefits plus dates kind of hook up."

"A relationship then?" Laughing at me again.

"No. Just a hook up after we have eaten or saw a movie or whatever we do beforehand."

"A relationship then?" Still laughing at me.

"No. I told you. Fuck. I have been duped haven't I?"

"Oh Yes! Well and truly."

"Ah Maaaaaan." Stamping my foot on the floor. "We still aren't telling people. We are just seeing where things go at the minute in case it doesn't work out. So please don't mention it as I aren't ready for questions and 'I told you so' and all that crap." Shaking my head at realising I have been conned.

"No worries. Did you look up the band Blackout?"

"N. Not yet why?"

"They're opening the bar, as you know, but also doing the music for the party. They are amazing you will get their vibe."

"Fancy a day of shopping?"

"We can't remember. Going to the bunkhouse."

"What you too? Why the urgency going to the office of scratch my itch. Is it to do with Boyo's?"

"I guess it must be."

"Well I aren't going. I am pissed off at him, even more so now I realise what the shits done, so no I am going shopping. You coming?"

"Well who am I to knock back a shopping trip?"

"YES. Give me 5 minutes and we are out of here."

ME: Sorry. Going shopping with Caitlin and can't make the meeting.

DICKWADD: Get your arses here for 11 or I will hunt you down (angry face emoji)

ME: Happy hunting arse wipe. Girls need to shop (Shopping bag emoji)

DICKWADD: Lenny I swear. If I have to hunt you down you won't sit down for a month! (Angry face emoji. Hand emoji)

ME: Whatever big guy. Caitlin and I are shopping. We need things for the party tomorrow night so fill your boots. Something's are far more important :D

DICKWADD: YES. Like this meeting. So help me God Lenny! (Fuming face emoji)

ME: (Angel face emoji) Toddles.

I turn my phone off lock up and head out for a shopping bonanza with Caitlin.

Chapter 34.

Spencer.

ME: Lenny has decided to go shopping with Caitlin (Fuming face emoji)

JAMMY: Typical

DONNY: Fucksake. She does my head in at times. Sister or not.

ME: We are still meeting. The party is tomorrow night and we need to put plans into action

JAMMY: McLane will be there :D

DONNY: Maverick will be there :P

MADDOX: McAllister will be there :)

ME: McAllister?

MADDOX: Couldn't think of a good one with M so went with Home Alone trooper Kevin

ME: (Crying laughing emoji)

Everyone piled into the bunkhouse just before 11 and got themselves comfortable. Donavan bringing sarnies and Jameson cakes.

"Your sister is going to be the death of me I swear!" I spew out to the guys.

"Tell us about it!" the guys say together.

"Look. Tomorrow night is the party and if the party crashers arrive we need a plan in place. They may want to try and lift her. So everyone please meet Crystal." As I introduce my saviour.

"Jameson you already know her. Maddox and Donny, Crystal is the one who attached my leg back on."

"Oh stop being so dramatic. It was a little cut." she plays it down but we know what a blessing she was.

"Jack, Nibble and Topez, already know her obviously. Now Topez is out on recon. Jack and Nibble are on route here and this is Johnson. Head of MI5 who is our unofficial back up."

"Unofficial?" Jameson frowning.

"Yes. Unofficially. We feel someone in his office is behind or at least involved in whatever it was Lenny got herself mixed up in. If that's the case, then we may not be enough. Johnson is here to unofficially lend us support. In fact Johnson and his crew are on a very earned holiday."

"Excellent. So what are we going to do with Lenny?" Donny questions openly.

"Crystal will double up as Lenny tomorrow night and when she needs to go out of the party, or travel home then Crystal will take her place. We are all staying over at the parents house anyway but she has the animals to look after so Crystal will take over that part and Jack will be waiting in the wings, holding the fort with Crystal till morning. If the pain in our arse decides to go home then obviously I will take her and cover from there. The problem we face is the costumes. We know there won't be any double costumes. If there are then security pounce and want confirmation they are who they are. There will be some high class people there tomorrow night, as we know my parents are well known, so it will need to be discretion at all times. Especially security."

"Will there be eyes everywhere?" Crystal intervenes,

"Yes. There should be. I have personally recruited people for the evening and with us on the floor too we should be able to keep her safe. We need to update Caitlin on the situation to. She is playing a blinder at the minute with Lenny and honestly can't thank her enough. She has tagged her with the spray so even if we lose sight of her we will still be able to keep tabs on her. So all areas are covered. HOPEFULLY!"

"Do we have the list of who is attending and in what costume?" Maddox asks,

"We will have it later after I have been to see the folks. All the decorations are being put up today and last minute fixtures all confirmed so I need the itinerary from her later. I will get it to you all as soon as I have it. That is my next stop from here. SO. let's plan!"

After finalising plans with all the group I head over to the parents. Pulling into the car port, the sight in front of me was like a nightmare. Vans dropping things off. Groups placing decorations everywhere. Mother watching with a smile on her face whilst world war three is unfolding in front of my very eyes.

"Mam. What is going on? I thought this would have all been sorted by now. It's a logistical nightmare. Where is the order?"

"Oh you worry too much. It is fine and all ahead of schedule."

"Speaking of the schedule. We need to talk." As I guide her out to grape vines out back she is looking at me with worry and fear.

"What's going on Spencer? You have that look."

"What look is that?" I play off with a smile,

"THAT LOOK." pointing to my face. " The one that tells me something is wrong but you are hiding behind that beautiful smile. Remember I am your mother and I know things." Linking my arm, "So tell me what is so important you need to walk me through the vines for because this is the only place you EVER tell me anything serious. It's always been your thing. Have you another mission you need to leave for?"

"No. Not leaving for one BUUUT I need your help."

"Anything. Tell me."

"Alright. Let me tell you a little story!" As I spill everything to the one woman in my life who always has my back. We walk for what feels like an eternity as I tell her all about Lenny. The trouble. How I brought her back to save her and how we are all going to do it.

"No problem at all my boy. Consider it done."

"Thanks mam. Remember,"

"I know. Not a word to anybody." She stops us walking turns to me and places her hands on my cheeks.

"I always knew you were special my boy." Kisses my cheek and walks back into the danger zone we now call Super Hero Ville.

Plans in order I make my way home and wait for Lenny.

WIFE: You home yet Dickwadd

ME: Yes. Want company

WIFE: Not this evening. I am still with Caitlin and we are heading to your mum and dad's to help with tomorrow. Your mum put an SOS out. Could you possibly keep an eye out on the animals. I have been and sorted them earlier for the evening. They just need checking on later?

ME: If I get eaten by a runaway goat I am going to tan your hide! (hand emoji)

WIFE: Tan as is false tan? News flash. I don't have any :D

ME: My hand and your arse whilst over my knee ><

WIFE: Oh yes please. But maybe tomorrow night eh :P Thanks Dickwadd

ME: I will dick you!

WIFE: Promises. Promises :D Thanks I owe you one (kiss emoji)

ME: I have a list don't worry :D

I go and check on the animals after I have checked over the footage of today. Houdini was at it again. I saw him jumping his pen wall and follow

Lenny after she had put the feed out for them and her marching him back in. She ended up picking him up and putting him back in with extra food. Creased over with the display of dominance FROM the goat. Too funny. I hop over the wall check all doors are secure and animals are down for the night. I don't need to worry about Lenny as I know she is staying at the parents house tonight. I head back home, sit out on the decking with a beer and watch the sun go down. I must have dozed off as I am jumped out of me sleep with a crashing noise. I quickly go in the house and collect my piece from the safe when I hear the carnage. Checking the monitors to see if I can see anything. Just a shadow.

"I must get that corner in shot!" Saying to myself. "Right arsehole let's see who you are!" I knock out the deck light and slowly slide myself round the wall. A quick look round the corner. No one there. I crouch down and run to the wall. I go to stand up and jump the wall Houdini hops over and runs to the deck. "That fucking goat!" I shout. "That's it. Your pen is getting an extension tomorrow or you're going to the butchers!" I leave him bouncing round my garden whilst I hit up the phone and she answers in three rings.

"Your goat is going to the butchers. I don't know if you eat goat but he is going!"

"You can't do that he is just excited."

"Then get him castrated. I just nearly shot him!"

"SHOT HIM!"

"Yes shot him. Heard shit unfold in your garden I was about to shoot whatever or whoever was there. Lucky for him he jumped over my head. If he was a cat he would be nearly out of lives by now. First a box hat now a bullet. Thin ice my friend thin ice!"

"You CANNOT shoot Houdini! Why would you shoot anything or anyone on my side anyway? What you expecting Whitesands Animal Mafia?" laughing at me.

"Very funny. I am building bigger walls for him or he can go in the dogs house and Pip can stay with me."

"You're pinching my dog now too? I think I need to re-evaluate this looking after my pets. First you want to shoot them. Then take them to the butchers THEN pinch my dog. I want a divorce."

"Not happening sorry. I would say it's either me or the pets but I know the pets would win so I will find another angle!"

"HMMMMMM I still want a divorce!" Blowing me a kiss she ends the call. I love this girl.

"Right Houdini. Let's see what I can do with you tonight shall we."

I pick him up and go back over the wall. I see the barn where she is going to be putting her horse and put him in there. Put some bedding down, food and drink in. "Try and get out of there pal!" close the bottom half of the barn door as even I know it's too high for Houdini and head home. Fucking animals!

Chapter 35.

Lennox.

After a very successful shopping trip, Caitlin and I head back to my house for a wine or three when Caitlin's phone rings.

"Hey mam you alright?"

"Hello baby. I was wondering if you could help me at the house. There are many people here trying to get sorted for the party tomorrow night and I could do with a little help. Fancy a girls night with your ma?"

"Yeah I can do. What time and what do you need?"

"Just you. I have everything here I just need a hand. I still have loads to sort. Where are you?"

"I am at Lenny's we were sorting the animals out then going to have take out and some drinks but we can bring the party to you if you want?"

"That sounds like a great idea."

"Fancy games and drinks at mom's tonight? She could do with some help with preparations? We both know that's code for pre party drinks."

" I am up for that yeah. I will shot some clothes in a bag and be right with you."

"Lenny's in too. We will be about an hour?"

"Excellent. See you soon."

"By ma."

"Oh this is going to be messy."

"I know. I can't wait." laughing too as I pack a bag and we head off to Caitlin's.

Reaching Caitlin's parents house armed with take out and many wine bottles, we head inside where her mum was directing the last few ornaments. Well, I say ornaments, HUGE statues. "Just in those two corners and you are finished." We hear her instruct.

"This place looks AMAZING. I forget how exciting your parties are. Cannot wait for tomorrow night if I am honest." Beaming at them both looking at me all excited.

"Well. It will be even more exciting now you are here too. You have missed so many so we may need a few more to catch you up to speed with what you have missed." she suggests. Even I know she is serious. If it's one thing Caitlin and my parents have in common. It's parties.

"So. Where do you want us and what can we do to help?"

"Ah it's fine and under control now I just thought a pre drinks games night was in order. You know I can't sleep the night before a party, so might as well start early. I will fetch the glasses, you two open the take out and put some tunes on I will be back in a blink." As she rushes out the room for the wine glasses.

"We totally saw this coming!" Caitlin giggled as she blasted out 80's tunes as I opened all the take out. Pizzas, parmesans, kebabs with bbq and garlic sauces to boot.

"Shit. Caits. I need to ring Spencer!"

"Why?"

"Because the animals will need a look over later so if I ask him to look over them I won't worry AND I know where he is." Wink, Wink.

"Oh tabs on him already," Caitlin laughs at me

"Well. Have you seen the guy?"

"YES! The Numbnuts my brother."

"Yeahhhhhh." Fluttering my eyes at her.

"And such a beautiful one too. But DO NOT tell him I said so because I am trying to still stay mad at him." laughing back at her as I ring up my sex toy.

"And how's that working out for you?" laughing at me, "Just message him. It will be quicker and we are partying so keep it short lady MOVE! MOVE! MOVE!" Clapping her hands to me. That's it. Totally creased.

Chapter 36.

Spencer.

Early next morning I head over Lenny's and let the animals out, put feed out for them, clean their beds and head back home with Pip. We go over the fields and check on the sheep and the outer areas of the land on the quad bike and tool kit. I fixed up a few fence wires that have came down and head home. Pip and I relax on the decking swing when I notice it's a little wobbly and a few boards are loose. I go to the tool bag and grab a hammer and a few nails. I raise a few of the loose ones and take the old nails out and secure them back in place. Well! Well! Well! I say to myself. I go and find my phone and dial up a group face time chat for the lads.

"Hey just wondered if you were all sorted for tonight?"

"These outfits show my best assets." Donny replies with a wink,

"Yeah? Mine leaves nothing to the imagination. Good job I am content with my manhood." Maddox chips in as we all laugh.

"Yeah. No hiding away from the girls this time Bro." I reply with a wink and a wipe of the brow

"One time guys! One time! I was ten and those girls were scary as hell."

"Yeah but waiting around secretly listening into their conversation seeing what they're planning next wasn't at all a little creepy?" They all nod understanding my point.

"Well what else was I supposed to do. They thought being my friend was great way for getting to you guys. Used I was Used!" Laughing uncontrollably we all say goodbye and I sat back down on the swing chair and waited for them to arrive.

Ten minutes later the guys pull up and walk over a few bottles in their hands and their gear for the evening.

"Hey guys. We starting this party early?"

"I always start early you know that." As Donny places none alcoholic bottles down on the deck as we all grab one.

"Caitlin mentioned you were animal sitting so thought we would keep you company." Jameson replies.

"So what time we getting their for tonight?" Donny asks.

"I aren't sure." I say as I put my finger to my lips for them to be quiet and let me speak.

"But you know ma." As I lift the board up and point, "She will be partying with the girls way before opening time. They were altogether last night as ma wanted a pre party." As they see the listening device under the board.

"Well if they're having a pre party so can we. Bottoms up guys." As we all tap bottles, blast the music and talk shite for the next few hours. We all shower and change and book the family car to collect us. Inside the house is clear. We all went through it with the devices that detects bugs and cameras. We keep the music on just for good measure and talk quietly with hand signals in the bathroom whilst the water is running.

"It is only a listening device with no camera attached. You can't get into this place with the pressure pads and alarm system, it's all clear in here but air on the side of caution. I need to have a relook in Lenny's in case there's a few in there that aren't ours. If the attempt happens tonight then we know it's him. If not then it rules him out. If it doesn't. They all know the set up and we have all the plans in place. NO ONE will touch a hair on her head. However, we still need to be on our guard in case the plans been intercepted. We ready?"

"Hell yes!" They say "Let's do this!" As Batman, Robyn, The Flash and Iron Man get into the hero limousine.

Chapter 37.

Party.

Pulling up outside mams house you can see security in full force. Some in sight some obviously hidden and some dressed as waiters. We head inside and it's a sea of superheroes and villains and is bouncing. Blackout, the live band, is situated in the garden terrace area and already have a crowd of dancers and they belt out 'Batman,' as strobe lights light the night sky in many colours and there in the centre of the dancers are Caitlin and Lenny. Where else would they be? With a drink in their hands and dancing away, they have never looked so happy. I go in search of the happy couple and find them in the kitchen doing shots.

"Seriously! shots? This early?"

"Ah relax my boy, it's only 3% strength, working up to the hard stuff later!" Winking at me as mam downs yet another.

"ALL RIGHTY THEN." As I prize them away from the shot table.

"Relax son." dad whispers, "It was lemonade. We won't be drinking tonight and if we do it will be none alcoholic."

"No dad I don't want you to be sober it's your anniversary and you both should be enjoying yourselves."

"Look son."

"No dad listen. Caitlin and Lenny are having a great time. We will be here to keep them safe as well as all the security. You two go and enjoy your night we have got this."

"That maybe so son." Mam chirps in "But we have your back as well as the rest of you. We are here to help and if SAID PEOPLE are even close by they will think it's alcohol flowing your father and I want to be sober and of sound mind so if they think we are drunk that's on them we are none alcoholics tonight and when this is over we can party again and besides, pretending to be drunk is way more exciting than actually being drunk. I had enough last night. My boy, we couldn't get up this morning. Good times." she kisses my cheek, pats my face and they both move to mingle. Probably back to the shots table. Bring on the show.

I make my way over to the girls spinning their arses around on the floor to the Time Warp now in full swing, dragging me into it to I don't mind. I can bust a move with the rest of them.

"Can I join you?" The Joker asks, aka Jared, Caitlin's partner and secret crush.

"Of course Joker. Bring on your best moves." Caitlin shouts as they start dancing I drag Lenny away.

"I hope you haven't shot my animals as you will wake up castrated tomorrow! And where are you taking me?" Lenny asks.

"To our favourite hidey-hole." I say with a wink "You haven't saw it for a long time, It's time you were reacquainted with it." Stopping dead on her feet

"Oh. Is that right? Well maybe I don't want too Quick Draw McGraw!" Laughing as I fling her over my shoulder.

"Ah like you think you have a choice Wife."

"AGAIN WITH THE FLINGING OVER THE SHOULDER! We have discussed this. Put me down numb nuts!"

"As you wish." Throwing her on the bed in my old bedroom and them jump myself right on top of her and kiss her.

"Ohh I have missed that sharp mouth of yours Baby girl."

"Shut up Dickwadd and carry on!" Grabbing my face and brings it down to hers were passion hits. Her legs wrapped round my waist. Pure bliss but so not the time.

"There's a party in full swing. I just wanted a sample of you before I couldn't drag you away again. Your lips are delicious. Have a good night last night? Mam said a few problems were happening this morning. You know not able to get up. By Lennox! Lennox! Lennox! Just how much did you actually drink to make my mother unable to get out of bed this morning?"

"Now that would be telling Doc Holliday wouldn't it? Us girls take an oath. No information here I am afraid. However, The recycling bin needs emptying." Swinging us round and now sat on top of me,

"Maybe you can prize it out of me later when I am drunk and tanning my hide over your knee! Sorry about going at it with you it was uncalled for and I apologise." She winks, kisses my nose and hops off me, turns at the door as she turns the handle. "But then again. You need to be man enough for that!" Running out the room as I jump off the bed to catch her. Laughing I make my way down to the party as a security guard comes to me and gives me an earpiece.

"This one is on a different frequency. We will know if anyone listens in on it."

"Thank you." I place it in my ear and carry on to the party in the garden.

Party is in full swing when the music stops and Mam and Dad make a speech. They're doing a cracking job in being 'drunk' They carry on the speech for a good ten - fifteen minutes giving us a chance to scan the areas, all clear for now. The game of the night starts. First group to crack the code for a case of champagne to the winner. Clues are hid around the garden and vineyard and it is a timed game. Caitlin, Lenny and Jared are a team. Some of us are at the clue points to help, strategically placed to see all areas and angles. All teams are given a number and time then off they went. The Joker, Cat woman and Batgirl head off in three different directions "THIS WAY!" Cat woman shouts.

"No it's this way!" Joker shouts back then realise their mistake laughing they group back together and then head the wrong way again. Batgirl stops.

"KAPOW, HIYAAA, BANG.. THIS WAY PEOPLE!" Batgirl yells and all three run off in the same direction.

"Oh boy this is going to be fun!" I tell Donny. Who is holding his sides crying with laughter.

"Fuck this is hilarious." He says as he is filming them on his phone. They were doing well and got round the course pretty quick when Lenny ran off.

"Targets on the move." Security relays. I move to see where she was going.

"Crystal you in place?"

"In situ boss. She has gone the bathroom."

"Targets in sight. Came through the vineyard want me to lift?" Security asks.

"Not yet hold tight. He hasn't attempted yet. Keep eyes on the target and prey."

Security responds, "He has followed her into the house. Dressed as The Penguin. Hasn't quite pulled it off. The Mayor has black shoes with white stripe. This guy white shoes black stripe. Keep an eye on the shoes Crystal."

Lenny enters the bathroom quickly followed by Caitlin. "Yoooo Bat Girl! We pee together remember. Wait for meeeeeeee. I need help with my cape." As they both stumble in the loo giggling.

Luckily it's the on suite and Crystal is in the room connected. As they go in the cubicle together Crystal walks out the room and takes her place. Walking down the stairs and through the main house and over to the vineyard where Mr Penguin had been hiding out as he follows her back out to there. Keeping her in view and on com's all the time as she heads to see who is on the leader board when Penguin strikes.

Chapter 38.

Crystal.

All of a sudden I felt the metal in my back. "Don't make any sudden movements smile and walk backwards. Don't look round!"

"It's alright Crystal we are here and moving in. Don't make any sudden movements like he said and do what he says till we reach you." I say quietly in her earpiece.

"Keep walking. Where is it?"

"What?" I say quietly so he can't make out my voice.

"The files where are they I need them NOW WHERE ARE THEY?" Dragging me further into the vineyard.

"What files I whisper?"

"You know what files. I WANT THEM NOW WHERE ARE THEY?" He turns and pushes me to the floor "Kneel!" he shouts, as he places the gun to the back of my head.

"He won't shoot you Crystal until he gets what he wants. Stay calm."

"I don't know what you mean!" Clicking the gun into position.

"NOW Crystal!" I hear Spencer shout I throw myself forward turn onto my back kick him in the balls, as he drops his gun to cradle his pain I stand up knee him in the face. Punch him in the side of the head and run like hell out of the vines. Spencer grabs me and lays me down on the ground whilst he kneels to see where he went. Security in his ear telling him he has ran the opposite direction and then onto a motorbike way and rode off the land.

"I got him good boss."

"That you did my little fire cracker and will you PLEASE call me Spencer!"

"Not today boss."As she stands and laughs at me as we make our way back to the house.

"Let's see what tomorrow brings hey?"

"Oh yes!"

Chapter 39.

Spencer.

"Oh that will be fun. Can't lift him yet till we have the rest of the gang. We need to know who the ring leader is because it isn't him. I still say it was him in the mall who you sprayed. He is still in the hide out, hopefully the transfer on your hand will stay on trigger happy tonight. Will check when I get back but you connected well." I say to Crystal, relieved she is alright I pull her in for a hug and kiss the top of her head as we walk back to the house.

"Oh it's on his boss don't you worry."

"Grounds are clear Mr Stone. Enjoy the rest of your evening. We are still patrolling and will be in touch if we come across anymore wannabe's. Bat girl and Cat woman are in the kitchen doing REAL shots with Joker"

"Thanks Mr Spice." As we laugh and head back in. Crystal heads upstairs the back way out of sight to change and help with the perimeter watch and I go and find the crazies in the kitchen. It's not long before the party was ending and there's just mam and dad, Robyn, The Flash, Cat woman, Bat girl, Iron Man and myself Batman in the study playing roulette for shots. A messy way to end the night. Jack and Crystal head to Lenny's to do a job for me and look after the animals and security was helping see off the last of the partygoers. The guys from Blackout came and had a drink with us as we talked about opening night at the bar. They stayed around a while and drank with us till their driver came and they headed off. Lenny was being a little off and cold I thought and not looking at me need to tackle this one when she pipes up.

"I thought it was one outfit only so no one doubled up tonight?" She puts out there.

"It was." Donny, also known as Robyn replied.

"Well unless my eyes were deceiving me I could have sworn I saw another Batgirl!"

"Have you had too much to drink sis?" Jameson, The Iron Man, pipes up,

"No. and if I aren't mistaken there must be two Batman's too as I saw your double over near the vineyard!"

"Yes definitely too much to drink sis."

"Bullshit! Who was she?" Turning and looking at me dead in the eye.

"Who was who?"

"FINE! If you're playing that game. FUCK YOU!" Pulling her phone from her bat boots. Taxi for the Stones residence please. She says as she walks away.

"Lenny wait."

"NO. You had your chance leave me alone and go find your other Batgirl. You seemed cosy enough." as she walks out to the main gate.

"Lenny wait." I shout but she ignores me as Caitlin runs past me, stops her and turns around to us all.

"This needs to sorting once and for all."

"Caitlin!" I say through gritted teeth.

"No Spencer." Leading Lenny back in the house "It needs to be done!"

"What are you talking about Caits?" Lenny questions.

"You will know soon enough." As we all walk back into the house.

She walks past us and into the house face full of thunder. "SHIT!" I say hanging my head.

"Let's go Batman." Iron man says with a pat on the back.

"She isn't going to like it."

"I know but it's time and this way she can help us help her!" As we both stop, look at each other and laugh when my phone beeps.

JACK: (Thumbs up emoji)

As I stop and show Tony Stark, high five each other then carry on walking in.

ME: OK emoji

We walk in and meet everybody in the study.

I stand there take a deep breath and look at Lenny.

Chapter 40.

Spencer.

"What is going on Spencer?" Lenny stands there arms folded and fingers tapping her sides.

"Look Lenny sit down. It's hard to have this conversation with all dressed like this. Let's just turn in for the night and rehash this tomorrow."

"NO! You spill now! Who was she and why are you all looking at each other like you're hiding something. You all have guilty looks on your faces. What's going on?"

"The person you saw dressed as you was Crystal. She was impersonating you tonight to filter out the mole in my organisation. Not just my organisation but MI5 too."

"Well what has that got to do with me?"

"August 2020 you were in Southern rain forest."

"I don't want to talk about that!"

"Tough. You want to know what is happening? THIS is what is happening! I was working as recon team with the Marines trying to infiltrate smugglers. We knew MI5 had a leak and we needed to find it. Can you imagine my surprise when we recon the area and find YOU of all people in it. You're group were trying to rescue animals before they were killed and smuggled out. What you weren't aware of was they knew all about you and you're group. You're knowledge of the area and the reason why you were really there."

"You have no idea what you're saying Spencer."

"YES. I DO! We were watching you watching them watching you. We also knew that someone in your own organisation was also working both sides. The evening of the 25th."

"STOP!"

"NO! The evening of 25th when the shit hit the fan. You took something from them that they want back. In fact they nearly killed you for it until we bombarded the camp."

"You have no idea what you are talking about Spencer. You have this all wrong."

"No Lenny I don't. A rival gorilla gang infiltrated the camp who was trying to take over the organisation and force them out so they had total control. They also knew you had what they wanted. They just couldn't find it."

"You are losing it Spencer. You weren't even there I would have known if you were."

"Wrong Lenny. Every time trouble landed at your feet I was there protecting you. You may have thought I hadn't seen you in years but in fact I have followed you around the globe. This camp wasn't the only time you were in trouble. You have been gathering information on animal smuggling for years. What you didn't realise was WE were right behind you. That night they broke into camp, tied your hands behind your back and blindfolded you. They made you kneel in front of them with a gun to your head."

"Stop Spencer. I don't want to hear it. I also have no idea what this has to do with 'Crystal' pretending to be me!" Lenny says through gritted teeth and watering eyes as her hands and toes tap. Obviously in distress of the evening events unfolding.

"Well that's where it is tough. You kneeled there with a gun to your head and just as he was about to pull the trigger all shit hit the fan. Someone charged the camp, which was my core, and we took down the majority of the cell. You were slashed across the back of your neck hoping to sever your nervous system cord then hit you to finish the job. What they didn't count on was me coming for them. I disarmed the man attacking you as we fought and I took him down he managed to get his hand free grab the machete knife and hit the back of my leg nearly taking it off. You at this point were out cold and bleeding but somehow I managed to get you to safety. Nibble and Jack got you to hospital. We weren't 'In the country' I was dragged out of the camp by who would become a great asset and my saviour. Crystal. She managed to get me to safety and worked on my leg. You were in a coma for a while. I managed to reach Jameson and flew him out to you that's why when you woke up he was there. Crystal sheltered myself and part of my team. I lost two good men that night but I managed to save the one person I care about most in my life. I watched you from a far as I healed. Had regular updates on you and made sure you came to no harm."

"It was you?" Shocked to the core, shaking.

"Look. That doesn't matter right now. We know the rest of the rival gang are here. We have taken one out already. We have had you under surveillance since you were home and then some before."

"You have been watching me?"

"Yes. Someone has always been with you, if not actually with you, you have been watched. We needed to find out where they were hiding as they need somewhere to take you if they lifted you. I needed them in my own back yard to fight them. That is why..."

"That is why you have made it impossible for me to not be anywhere else but come home!" realisation kicking in.

"Look at the bigger picture. We will go through that later."

"No. Now! You have been interfering with my life for years and I am supposed to be alright with this? Are you fucking crazy?" Lenny shouts as she stands up and points a finger at my chest.

"Sit down Lenny." Jameson shouts.

"NO!"

"YES! You have no idea what lengths people have gone to - to keep you safe now sit your arse back down and listen to the rest. We ALL. YES ALL, know what's been happening and it is MUCH bigger than what you think. YOU are just a little pawn in a big game of chess but you can also bring it down now shut up, sit down and listen!" As she sits back down Jameson goes, sits next to her and puts a protective arm around her shoulders.

"Once I was fit enough to go back to work again MI5 still didn't have their mole. We had an idea but still needed to play it out. Once you came back we knew they would follow so we set a few traps. The commotion in the mall when you went with Caitlin? That was us taking out an attempted lift. That also helped us to put a trace on the guy who was watching from a far to see if the lift was done. HE, we think, is the main link and head of the outfit. Crystal managed to bump spray him and we have now the place they're hiding out at. We have had our suspicions on who the mole is but needed confirmation and hopefully tomorrow will show us who. He attempted to take you tonight. which was actually Crystal."

"So you have him then?"

"No. We need to make sure. Crystal has marked him well and truly and tomorrow will prove very beneficial. There will be no way in hiding the bruising. If I am wrong? Then we are back to the drawing board, however, I don't think I am. You are staying here tonight. Jack and Crystal are at your place. We are all staying here."

"Just one question. When did I die and give you control of my life?" She snaps at me.

"Your safety is my priority and so are the safety of everyone here. Your parents are still on their cruise and won't be back for another few weeks so they are fine."

"Don't tell me. You organised THAT as well!"

"No of course not."

"We did." My folks say together.

"Excuse me?"

"We did. We entered a raffle to help the 'Prevention of selling rare animals', and they won. We needed a way of getting them out to safety so we went to gala and bought tickets to win the cruise. It just so happens your folks won them and off they went."

"Hmmm just like that? MARVELLOUS!"

"Look. I know this is a lot to take in but you need to play along after tonight that you know none of this. The next few days will dangerous as they will make their move for you and retrieve the hard drive YOU KNOW you have with all the information on that they want."

"I have no idea what you're talking about Spencer."

"Don't lie to me Lenny, you know it is pointless. The question I have to ask is WHY are you holding onto it? Why haven't you handed it over to MI5 or someone else. Have you even looked at it?"

"Looked at what?"

"Lenny. We are making a copy of it as we speak so you may as well tell me what is on there before I check it out myself. Don't look so surprised Lenny it is me you are dealing with here. You didn't think I would know where you hid it?"

"You are making a copy? What? How? Why? WHAT?"

"We are making a copy. Well Jack and Crystal are. So before I check it all out for myself do you want to share anything?"

"You are all in on this? What is wrong with you people!"

"Hey!" Donny shouts.

"You are our sister and we will do ANYTHING to keep you safe ANYTHING. Protecting you doesn't stop when you are all grown up. We do it constantly. We have each other's back all the time and that never changes. So get off your high horse and tell him what he wants to know!"

"I CAN'T alright! I haven't even looked at it. I stumbled across the smuggling ring a few years previously. Our group decided to try and gather as much information as we could to give to the authorities. We tried going to them first of all, only to find they weren't interested. It seemed like they were also on the take. By this time we were known by them. Then the heat came off us for a while and we managed to find them again in Southern Rain Forest. We had plenty of evidence already but we wanted the big guns. We were so close on finding out who the ring leader was when we were caught and all hell broke loose in the camp. I managed the evening before to download loads of files from their computer when I snuck in when people were sleeping. I thought they didn't know what I did and that if I had done anything I did it in the commotion to put them off that I had no idea I had taken anything. I thought I covered my tracks pretty well. I guess not."

"Fooling people into thinking you had no idea what you had done saved you a little time along the way. Even had a few of us fooled at one time. However, I know you better than anyone and your poker face has never changed."

"Where have you hid it sis?" Maddox asks but she stays silent. "Where?" he asks again.

"Don't worry Maddox we have it. If you are worried the house is bugged Lenny. It isn't. YOURS however is."

"WHAT!" Yelling at me and jumping to her feet. "You bugged my house?"

"It has been bugged a while. We needed to make sure you were safe at all times." Caitlin answers,

"You knew as well? When?"

"The day we went to the spa for the evening. They had already had live feeds in the pens, garden and surrounding areas. Just needed some inside."

"You actually nearly caught me if that makes you happy."

"Ohhh goody. Well done me. FUCK YOU SPENCER!"

"When I went in the car and said I felt something off. Was that it?" She asks Caitlin. As Caitlin nods.

"Yes." I reply "I hid in the larder cupboard. Got real up and personal with beans but yes you nearly caught me then I never managed to close the door in time."

"I KNEW IT! I knew something was off. I want ALL bugs taken out of my property by tomorrow!"

"No can do."

"Errrr YES you can do. Enough with this shit you are not watching my every move again. It's a violation of my personal space I want them gone NOW!"

"Sorry. Again no can do. This morning I found a listening device under my decking. Right at the spot we talk at. We then had to sweep through your house again to see if additional bugs were placed as well as ours and they were. No cameras just listening devices."

"CAMERAS!!!! CAMERAS!!! SPENCER, CAMERAS!" Looking at me as if to say people can see us.

"Look. We found the devices so we know they're listening in. We have traced the signal and it is going to their hide out so when now definitely know where they are."

"So go and GET THEM THEN!" Shouting up into my face.

"We can't not yet."

"Why not?"

"Because Lenny," Donny interrupts "We need the head of the snake or they won't stop coming for you. We need the whole lot of them."

"Since when did you become a spy?"

"Since Spencer trained us all."

"What the actual fuck!" She says sitting back down.

"I am living a nightmare. Am I actually dreaming right now? OUWCH." As she pinches herself. "I guess not! So let me get this straight. You have followed me around the globe. Bugged my house. Have me followed and constantly watched. Trained everyone to be spies. Made me come home without me even realising. Shifted OUR parents onto a cruise they THOUGHT they had won and making me care about you all over again was just a ploy to use me to get a gang of smugglers off the street?"

"NO. Well yes to some but you coming back was a little forced but us getting close again wasn't. I didn't want us to get close again till..."

"Ah so you don't want us to be close again well isn't that just dandy!"

"Will you shut up a minute."

"NO I won't actually. You have used me all this time for your own gains and you expect me to be alright with that. Open my arms out and say Ah it was in my best interests. Bring it in! Fuck off Spencer. You're breaking me all over again but THIS TIME YOU will break more than me. I have had it with this bullshit. I am going home!"

"No you aren't Lenny. You are staying here. They are still after you and US well we will revisit THIS situation." Pointing to us both. "After this is done. YOU aren't running anymore and you are ALWAYS going to be MY priority no matter how much you don't to be it is tough!"

"Right. let's all calm down for a minute," Mam states. "We have all had a full on night. Lenny, Geoff and Barbara are having the most amazing time so don't worry about them. Jack and Crystal are at yours this evening keeping the animals safe as well as your house. If anyone goes there tonight, they will get one hell of a shock, however, it won't be targeted as you are here and this gang know that so they are also safe. Nibble is now on hide out duty with Topez so nothing will happen tonight. We are all staying here so WE are all safe. It is time to turn in and we will plan next steps tomorrow morning. Goodnight everyone. You all know where your sleeping. It's like your little sleep over's all over again. You know your rooms get some shut eye. Breakfast is at 8 in the morning. Come on husband let's go to bed." With a wink they head upstairs leaving the rest of us together split off to our own rooms. Lenny tries to head to her spare room.

"Oh no you don't. You are with me tonight!"

"I don't think so. Leave me alone Spencer. You have done enough damage. I don't want to be anywhere near you." As she stalks off to her room. I watch her leave. Wait till she has settled down and take a chair and sit outside of her room. Caitlin has the adjoining room and messages me telling me she is staying with Lenny tonight and that I was free to stay in her room. Thanking her I told her I would be staying in the hall and make sure the windows are locked and I would see them in the morning.

NIBBLE: Thumbs up emoji

ME: Thumbs up emoji

Putting my phone in my pocket I feel it vibrate I take it back and it is a file that Jack and Crystal have sent over.

JACK: Something to read whilst you can't sleep.

ME: You know me well.

I sit there and look at what is in front of me. "Well would you look at who we have here! Gotcha"

As my phone beeps. Sinners and Turner face timing me. They must have something and accept the call.

"Looks warm in that mere forest my boys. Give me it chapter and verse!"

Chapter 41.

Lennox.

"How long have you been on this Caits? I can't believe you haven't said a word. I thought we were best friends and you hid this from me. WHY?"

"Because it was the only way to keep you and everyone else safe. The organisation you stumbled across Spencer had been targeting well before then. You can imagine his surprise when he saw you there."

"Who is this Crystal anyway? Is that why Spencer's leg is all torn up and scarred?"

"Yes. She nursed him back to health. If it wasn't for her, he would have died. It was an unsanctioned hit and basically MI5 didn't know they were there so all knowledge of them were hidden. Crystal was at the wrong place at the right time. They have told me most of what has happened not all."

"Nursed him back to health. What other little delights was she offering him on his death bed? How cosy!"

"Well for one it wasn't too cosy for him. Two she is like a second mother to him, a lot older than him and is the mother of the group. She came over to his team afterwards and has been a vital asset since. You have actually saw her."

"Really. When?"

"The night at the nightclub. The lady he was dancing with. That was her."

"Huh. Looked pretty cosy to me."

"No not at all. In fact I think Jack and Crystal have a little thing going on but are professional on the job at all times as far as I can tell. Look Lenny. All of this has been to keep you safe and bring down a massive organisation that will stop a lot of torture in the long run. It will also bring all those to justice as well as you being free from all this shit for good. But until morning we can't do anything so let's try and at least sleep."

"Alright Cait's. Goodnight."

"Goodnight bud."

"NOOOOO!" I shout as the gun is pointed to my head.

"Shhhhh Lenny it's alright just a dream it's just a dream shhh I am here." As Caitlin cuddles into me,

"I am going to be sick." As I rush to the bathroom and feed the porcelain God. Caitlin comes in behind me wets a flannel and holds it to my head.

"You feel better now?" she asks.

"A little. I am all churned up. I am hating this. I thought it was all over with Caitlin and now it's all back. Why can't they just leave me alone?"

"You know too much I guess. Even though you haven't looked at it they think you have. They know it hasn't been handed over so they assume you have it still."

"I need this to end." As I throw up the remaining contents of my stomach. We lay there on the bathroom floor holding each other whilst I cry.

I wake up just after seven and somehow back in bed. Caitlin was already up and fresh clothes are laid out for me to wear. I guess the infamous 'Crystal' brought them round. I hop into the shower and cry the last remaining tears I have get dressed and stomach in knots head down to breakfast where I see everybody waiting. Great!

"Here she is." Donny says.

"Morning DONNA." I say with a little sass,

"Ohhh someone's up for it today I see."

"And where is my saviour this morning huh? Scared is he and ran for the hills?"

"No. I am right here." Jumping out of my skin.

"Arsehole."

"Morning wife."

"Fuck off Dickwadd." Everyone just laughs at us.

"So. What is happening today then? Besides de bugging my house?"

"Not happening. They need to think they have the one up on us. They now know you're on to them. What they don't know is we also know they know."

"Look. I need to go back home. The shelter is finally bringing me my pigs tomorrow and a horse. I need to be there. Not just that the chic's are hatching so whatever your planning you need to factor in that I WON'T BE PLAYING!" He needs to realise that I have to keep him out of this and I also need to know if he definitely has the drive. If they know he is involved they're all in danger and I can't have that.

"Look. If you have what you think you have then your all in danger as well as myself. I can't handle you all being hurt. This isn't what I wanted. I just want to left alone." I didn't think I had anymore tears to cry.

"Look yes they know we know you have it, what they don't know is that WE now have it. The only people who know are Jack, Crystal and myself. No one else on the team does yet and that's how I want it to stay. At least till later when I force their play."

"RIGHT!" Maddox pipes up, " I am sick of hearing if you have it or we have it. If you have the drive WHERE THE FUCK WAS IT?"

"Her confident." I say.

"WHAT?" They all yell.

"How did you know Spencer?" I asked.

"Why do you think I started our little dress up war? I needed to be sure nobody disturbed the area and the only way was to cover it."

"Played me and sucked me in again!" I sit with my head in my hands. "I just.." and run to the bathroom again and vomit my breakfast. I just can't handle all of this possessiveness and organising my every move.

"Hey look." He says sat next to me on the floor, "I am sorry alright. Lenny I love you so much I can't bear to have anything happen to you. This is killing me. You have always been my priority ALWAYS and I will do anything to keep you safe."

"You are organising my whole life Spence. You are a control freak I can't live like that!"

"I aren't a control freak Lenny. Just need you safe."

"You know how deranged this looks?"

"Yes I do. I promise this will all be over soon." As I turn and vomit again,

"Spencer. You can't keep doing this it isn't right."

"It is right and will soon be over. Think what you like about me and my motives but it will always be you. Even after this is over, you won't be going anywhere ever again besides by my side. You got that Lenny. I aren't leaving you EVER again." he kisses my forehead "Now let's go and make a plan."

"Spencer. When I was away I..."

"I know Lenny. I know. But you helped the family escape for all the right reasons. In fact, we picked them up and got them out. They now have a new identities as they have given us accounts on the trade. See I know everything and what we are doing with you is no different than what you did for them."

"That's why I haven't handed anything in. I was so scared for them as well as myself."

"I know. Look, the rest Lenny can wait till later. Come on." As he took my hand and pulled me up from the floor. I brushed my teeth and followed him out just in time to see Jack and Crystal enter the house.

"Hello Lennox, I am Crystal I am happy to finally meet you." She gives me a hug and whispers "Loving you keeping him on his toes and kicking his arse. LOVE IT." kisses my cheek and goes to sit at the table. Oh I think I actually like her.

Chapter 42.

Spencer.

Jack and Crystal come by the parents house about 8:30 and sit with us round the large kitchen table and help themselves to breakfast as we talk.

"So. Later I will meet the guys at the bunkhouse and bring them up to speed but before then we need to get a few things sorted. This is the ring leader. Look familiar?" As Jack shares pictures around the table.

"No Way!" Jameson spews as his tea spills all over.

"I knew you would be shocked."

"I can't believe it. He just doesn't ring bad guy does he?"

"No. He is definitely calling the shots and the reason we can't find anything on him and him thinking he has been one step ahead. Well not anymore."

"Let me see." Lenny asks. "I don't know him who is he?"

"THAT my wife, is Johnson!"

"WHAT THE???" Jameson says still in shock

"One. I aren't your WIFE and two. Who is Johnson?"

" Johnson my wife, is the head of MI5's smuggling ring division!"

"I can't believe it Spencer. How did we miss this? Hang on you just said him thinking he was one step ahead. You knew?" Donny enquires.

" We" pointing to Crystal, Jack and myself have known a while. We have been doing our own Intel on him. We just needed that last bit of proof It makes sense now though doesn't it Donny?."

"Yeah I guess it kind of does. Shit! So what's the plan. I promise I will listen as soon as the shock has worn off!" Sitting there in disbelief.

"So, Course of action. We need to wean him out. HOWEVER!"

"No. We don't like HOWEVER's!"

"However. Sinners and Turner were in touch last night and actually know who the main front man is." As he shows us the picture.

"Wait shouldn't we wait for Nibble and Topez? Hang on a minute WHAT?"

"I will bring them up to speed later. At the minute they're on a kind of quest." Winking at us all.

"As I was saying, we need to wean him out. They don't know we have the drive, so that's an Ace in our pack. If we let the other 'TEAM' in on the whereabouts we think it is, we may drive them out. I can't let them know in that meeting. However, if they over hear me talking about it to Lenny, in your house." Pointing to Lenny "Then that maybe enough. We need eyes on the ground and the drive back in the hole."

"It's already in boss. A copy of it is not the real one." He says smiling at me,

"Do I want to know what's on THAT one?" laughing at Jack,

"Let's just say Johnsons favourite hits." With a wink and as soon as it is opened it will automatically send the contents to MI5.

"Right hold on a minute. What is with the winking? It's all you guys do. It's ridiculous!" Lenny says.

"It's a guy thing," Donny chirps in.

"Whatever. Anyway crack on. Plan Go! Go! Go!"

"Listen to her now. Wasn't like that last night sis was it?" Jameson laughs.

"Right as I was saying. We need a way to wean them out and go for the drive, the only way is like I said over hear us. So Lenny you and I are going to put on a little showdown at your place later. They will be listening in and take the Intel back to Johnson. He won't want anyone else going for the drive as he doesn't need anyone else seeing what is on it. We also need the crew out too. Once we have Johnson with the drive we can pick them up and take them in. Have you sent it over to our friend yet Jack?"

"Yes. It is all there including his favourite hits. They won't move till we give them the heads up." Jack says,

"Who has a copy and what now?" Lenny asks,

"No matter yet. I will call the guys to the bunkhouse later when Lenny and I have had a showdown. They will have all their information by then and will be plotting. Once I am out of the way they will try and lift her. That's when we will be waiting in the wings. So gather round, listening ears on, here is what's going to happen." As we go over the plans and leave.

Chapter 43.

Lennox.

"Hello my babies. How's my animals today. Sorry I have been busy but tomorrow you are getting new friends. YEYYYY." I tell the goats and chickens.

"What MORE animals?" Spencer groans.

"What's your problem Spencer, they're mine not yours and I will have as many animals as I want. They're transporting them here tomorrow. You're more than welcome to help me settle them in." As I kiss his cheek just for good measure.

"Sorry wife. That's a no can do. I have things on."

"Yeah like what?"

"Heading over to BOYO's with the guys to have the finishing touches sorting. The place opens in like four days it needs to done so Jammy has enlisted us in. To be honest I would much rather be there than here with Dr Doolittle's crew. I actually have so much work to be getting on with but bar needs to be ready!"

"Dr Doolittle! Cheek of it. You work! PFFT Haven't seen you do any since I have been back"

"I will show you work." Flinging me over his shoulder and then sits me on the table.

"You ready?" He whispers. I gently squeeze his neck and bring his lips to mine.

Stopping the kiss "When are you going to tell me about your nightmares?"

"What nightmares?"

"You know exactly what nightmares. You had another one last night!"

"Spencer it has nothing to do with you. Leave it alone!"

"No. I won't. Why won't you tell me?"

"Because I don't want to alright!" Pushing him away from me as I stand up back on the floor.

"You want to know everything. Control everything I do. I turn around and your there I can't BREATHE for you."

"Lenny!"

"NO. Don't you Lenny me! I am sick of it. I appreciate you looking out for me and helping with the animals but we need to slow things down Spencer. I can't take a breath when your here. You over crowd me and I need my space."

"Look after you. LOOK AFTER YOU! YOU have NO idea what I have done for you Lenny!" As he turns and walks away,

"WOAHH Hold up there Jackass. What do you mean WHAT YOU HAVE DONE FOR ME? What exactly HAVE you done for me?"

"Nothing forget it."

"No." Running in front of him stepping him from leaving.

"Tell me what the hell you are talking about. I come back and you're in my face constantly. One minute your here the next minute your where I am going. It's like you have tabs on me or something EVERYWHERE and I mean EVERYWHERE I GO you seem to be there or one of your cronies is. Don't think I haven't noticed Spencer. You are becoming overbearing I can't move without you!"

"Lenny look."

"Lenny, Lenny, Lenny is all you say how about some answers Spencer!"

"Answers you say. You're a right one to talk about answers. Why not dish me some of yours and I will dish you some of mine?"

"Leave me alone Spencer alright just leave."

"No I don't think so. You want answers Let's go. How did you get the scar on your neck? Oh that was when someone knifed you! What are your nightmares about? Oh being nearly murdered in the Rain Forest! What happened in the rain forest? Oh you fell across a smuggling ring! How did Jameson get a call to say you have been seriously injured and needed to get over there ASAP in case you DIED! OH THAT would have been me!"

"WHAT! How did you even know about that? I didn't even know you were still in contact!"

"We never stopped Lenny. He is my best friend and the brother of my wife. Do you think we would just give up on each other?"

"ONE I AREN'T YOUR WIFE!"

"Yet!"

"ER EVER! And TWO How on EARTH did you know all of this was happening?"

"Who do you think saved you Lenny huh????? ME! Me and MY team saved your arse and your groups. I also know they're coming after you for the drive you took!"

"What drive?"

"You know exactly what drive I am talking about. The one with all the incriminating data, photo's, book logs EVERYTHING on it."

"I don't know what you are talking about. I can't do this Spencer. We are done. Over. Get out! JUST LEAVE!"

"Nice try this ends now Lenny. Where is the drive? I need it so I can't put an end to this and have you safe. I can't keep you safe if I don't know who I am up against. I need to know Lenny. NOW! They WILL come for it and you!"

"WE ARE DONE! LEAVE!"

"The drive Lenny, where is it?"

"I don't know what you are TALKING ABOUT LEAVE ME ALONE AND GET THE HELL OUT!" Spencer storms out, slams the door and I go and cry again on my bed and ring Caitlin.

"Hey Cait's you have a minute to talk?"

"Always gorgeous, what's up?"

"Your brother."

"I am on my way."

Caitlin took about five minutes to make it to mine runs in and up the stairs and lays besides me.

"What has he done now?"

"I can't believe it Cait's. I really can't."

"Believe what. What has he done?"

"Can I tell you something in confidence and it goes absolutely nowhere else?"

"Of course you can. you know you can tell me anything and it will go the grave with me. Are you finally going to tell me what has been happening?"

"Yes. When I was working around the world helping endangered species, my group came across a smuggling ring. "

"What!" Caitlin says shocked, she is playing this like a pro.

"We came across a smuggling ring. We tried reporting it to the local police but nothing was ever done but they moved camp. So when they did, we did. We kept following them, releasing animals when we could. Gathered pictures and things on them the works. What we didn't realise was they were onto us. One night I slipped into their camp when they all slept and downloaded loads of information from their computers onto a drive. I don't know what's on it I haven't had time to see any of it yet but that night after I got the information, the camp was raided."

"Lenny, No. Why did you put yourself in that much danger?"

"Cait's I wasn't thinking of me I was trying to protect the animals. Only it wasn't just animals. They were killing the animals and using them to transport drugs to neighbouring countries. When they landed at their destinations they would take out the drugs then sell the animals to collectors. I just needed proof. I thought if I had it and showed it to the authorities then it would shut them down."

"So what did you do?"

"I didn't get chance to do anything. I ended up in the hospital and then eventually came back home."

"So where is the drive. Do you still have it?"

"Yes. I copied it again when I got home and sent it to the MI5 authorities. I can't remember who I sent it to but I did tell them I have the original as well as the copy they have."

"Where is the drive now Lenny and does Spencer know?"

With a shaky voice, "Confident has it. And No I haven't told Spencer. What am I going to do? I have kept this all this time to keep him away from me so I didn't drag him into my mess and TADAAA He was the one who saved me from being killed. Go figure. What am I going to do Cait's?"

"It's alright Len. We will figure it out. Try and have a nap. The boys are at the club finishing off for opening night. I will stay with you."

Caitlin stayed with me till I woke up and had some lunch when I suddenly stop.

"What is it Lenny. What have you remembered?"

"I have remembered who I sent it to!"

"You do. Who?"

"Someone called Bailey."

"First or second name? No idea just Bailey."

"That's great Lenny. We need to tell Spencer."

"No. I can't involve him anymore don't you see. I can't let them get him too."

"Come on Lenny, let's get the stables ready aren't your pigs and horses coming tomorrow?"

"Yeah how did you know?"

"You told me at breakfast this morning woman!"

"God. I am forgetting everything I have no idea what is wrong with me!"

"WORRY! That's what's wrong with you."

"Quite possibly!" As we head outside and muck in.

"Come on Brave heart let's go do some work."

"Right with you Hamish,Chapter 44.

Spencer.

I make my way to the bunkhouse and secure Jack and myself inside. MI5 rings us in and I put it up on the big screen.

"Hey Derek. How's the family?"

"Doing alright. Howdy Jack you doing alright?"

"Cracking Derek. I sent over something for you to check over last night. You had time yet?"

"Oh yes. This is why this conversation is happening now. What's the state of play your end at the minute?"

"Lenny has mentioned where she has stashed the drive so give them a few hours to figure that out but we are on alert. How do you want to play this?"

"I am coming your way tomorrow. I have sent extra men your way." As pictures of the agents come up on the screen. Agents Wise and Zaff. They're two of my trusted men and will touch down at the airport in twenty. Thought you could use them with Turner and Sinner on 'Holiday' I have brought them up to speed and will take over the house watch of our little gangland wannabe's which will free up Nibble and Topez. Speaking of. They clocked in yet?"

"Yes they're on their way here now."

"Good. Keep me updated and don't forget. I know nothing."

"No problem. Speak soon." I cut it off Just as Nibble and Topez walk in.

"Morning boys I don't have long I need to get to BOYOs, help the guys finish off the place. Anyone seen Johnson and his men?"

"No not this morning. Probably off on a lead. You know Johnson plays his cards close to his chest."

"Nice shiner Topez. What happened to you?"

"Got in to something earlier. All good though it's sorted."

"What happened?"

"Followed one of the goons and he clocked me. I played it off as I was going to rob him so I didn't blow my cover. We had a rumble he got a lucky punch in he came worse off."

"Good job your quick thinker Topez." I tell him, "We have developments listen up."

"All ears boss."

"Lenny has told Caitlin where the drive is. The only problem is we now need to figure it out. She also sent a copy of it to the authorities. A Mr Bailey of MI5. Lenny still has the original SOMEWHERE but I know it will come to me. She knows we saved her arse in the forest, well, that we saved her but she still won't cave."

"How come she told Caitlin and not you?"

"I don't know. I think the blow out between us unnerved her and she needed to talk it out and who better than her best friend."

"So where has she stashed it?"

"It's with confident." I say with I have no idea shrug.

"Confident? Who is that if it isn't Caitlin?"

"I am wracking my brain but coming up empty. Just keep doing what we are doing and it will come good. She is expecting her pigs and horses tomorrow. MORE animals, it's like a mini farm over there I just hope we can get her out of this alive for her to enjoy her dream a little longer."

"She will be fine boss. She has us in her corner."

"Thanks Topez. We all know what is happening today whilst I go with the guys?"

"Yes. Go and help the boys. We have Lenny covered."

"Thanks Topez I appreciate it." I hug him out and then Nibble.

"Phones attached to me. Ring with any developments." I leave them there as I head to Boyo's.

"How's it going Spence? About time you got here. How's my sister?" Maddox asks.

"A pain in the arse. Let's get this bar done shall we!" Put the music on and work away. I swept over the bar. One listening device in the light. They make it too easy. Pointing up to it.

Maddox carries on. "I noticed what you did with your cape earlier. How is Gordo ever going to live this fashion disaster down. Caitlin must be cursing this battle your having."

"Nahhh she is loving it just as much as we are. In fact she has put a few things on him herself."

"Jesus, your games are hilarious. Remember when she was little she would go and tell him all of her problems. She would sprawl all over that bluddy gargoyle and spew out all of her secrets and worries and even tell him what we did. The secrets that Gordo has and could tell eh?" As we all start laughing.

"Yeah. We used to rinse her over it but she is a nutter so took it well. She is a crazy one and very unpredictable but we love her all the same." All agreeing and crack on with the rest of sorting of the bar. We manage to get it all finished ready for the cleaning crew tomorrow however we like to keep things open.

"Well guys we are almost sorted. Back again tomorrow? It should only need a few more hours and be ready for opening." Jameson asks.

"Count me in. Have a few errands to run and check in with the guys and see how we are doing but I will get round to help."

"Thanks Spence. How about going to PAP's tonight. We can ask the girls too?"

"Well I certainly need a drink especially after today's fight with your sister. Don't think the girls will come out of spite but I am there."

"Count us all in. We will get the girls to come no worries."

"Alright. Good luck and see you all later." I reach the car as my phone goes off and it is Agent Wise letting me know they're in place and ready. I shoot over a quick message that I am heading home and will check in later. I pull into the drive way and notice Lenny and Caitlin's cars still there, leaving them to it I let myself into my house pull a beer out of the fridge and watch the camera footage. I can see they're in the front room watching TV. Looking over the feeds through the house and grounds, I see all is quiet I go and jump in the shower. It feels like an age since Lenny and I were together. I picture her sat on that table today kissing me. I take myself in my hand and start to pump up and down. One hand keeping me steady on the shower wall I picture her lips around my cock, my hand round her head guiding her head back and forth. Before I know it, I am emptying myself with a moan into the running water. I place my head on the shower wall and let the water wash over my back when my mind moves onto what lays a head. I quickly wash and get out of the shower. Wrap a towel round my waist and lay on the bed and before I know it I wake up with the sound of Lenny screaming. I jump out of bed through on some shorts pick up my piece and run.

"LENNYYYYYYYYY!" I shout running to her screams and jumping the fence.

"LENNY TALK TO ME! WHERE ARE YOU?"

"SPENCERRRRRR." I hear her yell as I hear a car skid and spin away.

"FUCK!"

I run back to the house and look at the feed. "SHIT! Come On! Come On! Come On! Show yourself you bastards!" I rewind the feeds. "There you are." Ringing the troops,

"Black Mercedes. No plates. Two guys both around 6ft. Just took Lenny and Caitlin. Heading South maybe towards the hide out GO NOW." I ring Jameson

"They have them. They just took them heading to the Hide Out now Black Mercedes no plates two guys about 6ft. I can't believe I let this happen. I fell asleep on the bed I shouldn't have allowed this to happen."

"Spencer. You are exhausted. You have hardly slept. We thought she was safe. They won't be harmed we are on our way. Who will be watching Gordo?"

"Jack and Crystal are heading this way now meet you up the house."

"Spencer they will be fine don't panic."

"Easier said than done. I can't let them hurt her again Jameson I just can't."

"They will be fine see you in five."

I have changed into jeans jumper and jacket. Put my vest on and I high tailed it out of the house and into the car heading South. I pull up behind Wise and Zaffs vehicle and let myself in the back.

"They have taken them in. There's five guys in total."

" Is Johnson in there?" I ask,

"We can't be sure. We only know the ones going in. They were the two from the restaurant scar face and his cronies."

"Alright. All available people are her on comms, here are yours," as I hand then their ear pieces, "Let's go!"

"Nibble round the back. Wise cover the left side. Zaff cover the entrance from behind the far wall signal when ready. Jameson, Donny and Maddox keep on the outskirts in case any make a run for it. Keep out of the way of any fire. You in position?"

"Copy that." They all come in one after another.

"Hang fire I am getting audio from inside." Wise whispers. Channel three. All change to channel three. Who is that?"

"THAT my friend. Is the wife. You little beauty. She managed to keep in the earpiece. That's my girl. Remind me to propose to my girl after this guys!"

Chapter 45.

Lennox.

As soon as Spencer left I was on the phone to Caitlin. Knowing she will be play the game as well as be followed. Spencer left me the ear piece knowing we would be lifted at some point. I just need to remember to wear it. After the animals were sorted we headed back inside for a snack when we noticed Spencer's car was back which means one thing. The traps been set. We head inside and prepare ourselves for what's about to start. In no time at all we walk back into the house when I was grabbed from behind. "Don't react Lenny!" I keep thinking to myself "Not yet."

"Leave her alone!" I shout .

"She has nothing to do with this." I jump on his foot and manage to run to the kitchen worktop. He grabs me again pushes me to the work top and pins me over the kitchen counter "BINGO." I say to myself. I land make sure I land with hand under my chest allowing me to pick up the earpiece that I landed on. I turn my head to left secretly placing it in my ear as he pulls my hair back stretching my neck backwards.

"Nice try bitch. Let's go!" As she ties my hands behind my back and lifts me clear off the ground. They fling us in the vehicle.

"SPENCERRRRRRRR!" I manage to scream out to let him know they have taken us. We are then gagged and blind folded. The journey took ten minutes. So they must be holding up close. We stop and picked out of the car, walked into a building sat down on a chair and tied to it. They take the blindfolds off and there's Johnson along with his little cronies.

"What do you want from us?" Caitlin asks. Please let us go. We don't even know you. What do you want?"

"Caitlin, shhh it's alright," I say whisper, "SHHH stay calm."

"OHHH. Calm you say. Do you know how CALM I have been waiting for YOU to fuck up and lead me to what YOU stole? A long time pretty lady LONG TIME. Now tell me where it is and maybe just MAYBE you will live through this!"

"Nothing? Absolutely nothing? Is that how this game is going to played? We know EVERYTHING that is happening. We know where you have hid it. We know what you have been doing all of this time. You don't think I paired up with Stone all this time just to help stop a 'Crime lord' did you? Silly, silly little girl."

"Well if you didn't want to stop a 'Crime Lord' as you put it WHY did you?"

"Because you stole what was ours and now we want it back. The only way we knew for sure you had it is if we kept tabs on you. Spencer doesn't know a thing. He is so blinded by wanting to protect his little female he lost sight of the mission. To take down YOU and save our business."

"You keep saying OUR. Who is the OUR? You make out you are some high flyer but really your just the gofer. Is that what your telling me? You're the little message boy. The one who fucked up his bosses operation? Well sorry about that. I don't talk to the little people. I only deal with the boss. So until he is here. I aren't saying Jack shit!"

"Oh you are a right mouth piece I give you that. Not the scared little woman we came across in the forest."

"You're damn right I aren't. I aren't scared of you, your cronies OR your boss. I stopped your little organisation once. I will do it again if you DON'T LET US GO!"

"And how can you do that?" Johnson questions. Clearly on edge. He isn't the main ma. Who the fuck is then?

Johnson walks up to me "Mouth piece let's quieten you up a little eh, see how tough you are!" SMACK! Johnson slaps me across the face. I taste the blood coming from my lip.

"Oh that's hard of you. Feel like a real man now do you?" I goad him.

SMACK across Caitlin's as she yells "Arsehole! Feel better now do you?"

"Look. Do Not tempt me anymore than you are doing. This will end badly for you if you don't tell me where the drive is!"

"OR! It will end badly for you if I don't!" Spitting blood out on the floor making sure I hit his polished shoes. "If you have been listening and watching me then you will KNOW where it is, or are you that much of a shit operative you literally are a thick fucker? If that's the case. No wonder you are the gofer. I want to be hit by a better man not a pussy!" SMACK! Another crushing blow to the face. I feel my eye swell instantly. I have managed to keep him busy enough for me to untie my hands. Caitlin nods to let me know she has also unravelled her hand. "Like I said PUSSY. Where's the big guy? I aren't saying another word till I see him!"

"I AM the big guy."

"REALLY! I would have thought if you were the main guy you would have more than these four lousy armed men at your beck and call. Doesn't the 'Top Man' have more security. Like I said you can't be that important."

SMACK! "Keep talking lady. I can do this all day!"

"I mean..." Spitting blood at his face. "I mean hand guns? come off it! I would have at least thought rifles, shot guns or knives!" As one of the men draws out his knife.

"Oh I stand corrected. That's some serious knife your mate here has." I feel another back hander across my face as the earpiece flies out of my ear.

"NOW!" I shout as all hell breaks loose. Caitlin and I swing the ropes round hitting two guards across their faces and we hit the deck out of the way of gun fire. It all happens so fast I didn't even see what was unfolding in front of me. All I see is Nibble jumping through the far window at the back of the house picks me up and flings me out of it when someone else, who I have never saw before picks up Caitlin and launches her out the window seconds after me. We get up and run towards the trees when we grabbed by Donny, Jameson and Maddox and brought to the floor. "SHHHH." They say as the put their hands over our mouths. "Ouch," I yelp.

"Which one?" Maddox asks, "Johnson!" I say "Don't worry I will have my time with him. Even if I have to beg Spencer to let me at him."

Chapter 46.

Spencer.

Hearing Johnson hit her is fuelling my anger. I am pacing up and down. Boiling with every step. She is giving us the lay of the land and situation in there but her getting beat up wasn't part of the plan.

"NOW!" I hear her yell.

Nibble is the first through the back window. I hear Lenny screaming as she is thrown out. He takes out one of the assailants with a blow to the head from the butt of the assailants own weapon. Wise is next though his area and throwing Caitlin out the same window. He takes a shot to the arm, turns round shots dead one as two more flea through the door. "Jameson two heading your way. Maddox, Donny the girls." As the rest of us invade the building. Zaff gives chase to the two running as the split. Jameson runs after one and Zaff the other. I reach Johnson in three strides punch him twice to the face. I see the gun pointing my way I drop to my knees. I take the knife from my boot and throw it to his wrist. Direct hit. Gun goes off through the window, as I take my gun out fire at his shoulder. Well killing him straight away isn't any fun. He drops to the floor and I run to him kicking him to the side of the head. "That's for Lenny and Caitlin you bastard and good night!" Knocking him clean out. I turn him over, pull out the knife from his wrist and handcuff him and I drag him out across the floor like a sack of potatoes and fling him in the back of van. MI5 secure the area as they take out the body from the holdout, as Jameson and Zaffs walk back the two who ran one handcuffed the other at gun point, They are taken by MI5 as they tie Johnson to the ambulance bed. Donny and Maddox come over with the girls when Lenny runs and flings herself into my arms. Her face is a mess. "Lenny I am sorry. You should have..."
"Where is he?" she asks,

"In the ambulance." As she lets go and walks over to where he is being looked at.

"Can you give her a few minutes please?" As I instruct the personal to look the other way as she enters the ambulance and stands over him. Gripping his shoulder wound as he yells with the pain and with some force she raises her other hand and pummels the shit out of his face. "That's enough Lenny." I drag her away from him. "That's enough. Save some for later." I pick her up and take her out of the ambulance kicking and screaming at him.

"He kept saying ours. He can't be the main man Spencer. He can't be. Who is then?" she asks me

"Don't worry for now. I need to get you to hospital come on."

"I am fine Spencer you're not answering my question!"

"I need you to be looked after Lenny. We will talk about this later PLEASE let me take you and Caitlin to be checked over. Wise needs a Dr let's go."

"It's a through and through Spencer, I will live." Wise replies.

"That being so. I still need you patched up. Come on let's go and THANKYOU. You too Nibble just THANKYOU."

Within Ten minutes we were all in the local hospital. Wise was stitched up and released within a few hours. Lenny and Caitlin had face x-rays and were clear, Lenny's hand however had broke when she pummelled Johnson's face to beyond recognising. That's my girl. So she needed a plaster cast on and a sling to match which didn't bode too well. Suck it up lady. We all made it home a little after five and all piled into Donny's as it was the closest house. All exhausted we just crashed where we landed. Not able to sleep much I looked in on Lenny and Caitlin curled up against each other in the master guest bedroom and made my way downstairs to a fresh smelling pot of coffee.

"Can't sleep either?" I hear Donny say.

"You know me well. You can't either I guess. What's on your mind as if I need to ask."

"I can't get it straight in my own head. It was over within minutes yet seemed slow motion in every way. I hated the fact that they got hurt and I was so far away to help."

"You did good Don."

"How did you know which way they would run?"

"We strategically threw them out of that one knowing they would run directly your way. It is why I ask you both to cover that area. We knew the glass would fall inside the building so the landing outside wouldn't be to catastrophic. A few bumps and grazes but that would be it. Knowing you two where there made it easier to execute the rest of the plan without fearing the worst for them when they did run. I hate the fact they were hit I can't get it out of my mind. I want to kill the bastard!"

"Me too!"

"Hey. Anymore coffee for us?" As Jameson and Maddox appear from the kitchen onto the veranda.

"Certainly is my pals. Help yourselves. Fresh pot just made. So what's next?"

"Well. We now need to smoke out the big guy. Hopefully he has made a play. He is on his own now we have his crew. No doubt he will have been watching last night's show so now it is trying to figure out his next move." For the next hour or so we run through scenarios,

"Hey sleepy head. Wake up." I kiss the one place on her face that isn't cut, bruised or swollen. "Lenny wake up I have coffee." As I woft it in front on her nose.

"HMMMMM COFFEE. You really know how to wake a girl don't ya." she tries to smile then grimaces at the pain, "Ow. My lip feels like it the size of a golf ball."

"Go careful baby. Sit up slowly." As I help her up.

"Where's Caitlin?"

"She is downstairs with the guys and MI5 giving her account of what happened. They want to speak to you next. You up for it?"

"Yeah. Just as soon as I have attempted to drink this beautiful nectar." She attempts to drink and drips down her chin. "No. Spencer I can't drink it."

"That's why I brought you this." and hand her a straw,

"Ah you delight you." As she drinks her coffee and heads downstairs.

After Lenny gave her accounts of what happened Donny dropped us off at home and I carried her in to the house. Relieving Jack and Crystal.

"I can walk Spencer. I aren't ill!"

"I don't care. You are not moving a finger. Right sofa or bed?"

"Kitchen please I need to try and eat something I am starving. You?"

"Yeah I could eat a horse. Speaking of. What time the animals arriving?" We look to the door and there is Pip sitting there waiting head hanging. I walk over to her. Pick her up and bring her slowly to Lenny when her tail starts flapping and she carefully licks Lenny's face. Her plaster cast back to her face. Lenny sits on the window seat as I place Pip next to her. I go and get her a treat and run back to them.

"There you go Pip! Well done girl." I stroke her head and she lays on the seat with her head resting on Lenny's legs as Lenny's eyes begin to water. I kiss her head and set about making dinner. I make my way to the fridge and see Crystal has already made some sandwiches and has soup already made on the hob. I warm the soup up and pour us some out and place the sandwiches and soup on the table.

"I don't want to disturb her Spencer. She is so settled. In the cupboard left of the hob there a fold up table. Can you get it for me please?"

"Sure. This one?"

"Yes. Thank you."

"Don't rush your food. Soup is only luke warm so it shouldn't burn you. Take it slowly and if you can't eat the sandwich at least dip the bread till it is soggy enough to eat.

"Yes Sir!"

"Anytime Squire. Now eat!"

After lunch Pip took herself outside. Tail between her legs and very carefully. Once outside she turns and gives a little bark as if to say 'see you later,' and candidly walks away.

"She is finding her bravery isn't she?" I ask Lenny,

"Yes. We have been working on it. She is doing so much better in such a little bit of time."

"She really is. I am impressed."

"Sheeesh training a dog impresses you and here I thought it was my mad sex skills!"

"Oh those as well." As I wink and take the plates and bowls to the sink and she comes behind me undoes my jeans with her good hand and places her hand in my boxers.

"As much as I really want you right now. You aren't ready. You're body has gone through a trauma just last night and I aren't the kind of person to take advantage of that." Fuck me this is hard as well as being hard. "The only place your going is the shower not bed. Well not yet anyway." I lock the door, pick her up and take her to her bathroom. Her shower room has a bench to sit on within the cubicle, which could hold a party of ten it is that big. I place her in the shower and carefully take off her clothes quickly followed by my own. I turn on the shower to a warm setting and moving her bench under the light stream keeping her poorly plaster cast hand and arm out of the way. I gently lather up the soap and start washing her. She starts to play with me with her good hand making me instantly hard.

"Lenny. Be careful. I can only hold off for so long." She continues to stroke my shaft every now and again licking the pre cum from the top.

"Lenny. I only have so much self control. Fuck that's good."

"I need to feel you Spencer." Taking all of me into her mouth. I rinse the bubbles from her body, take myself out of her mouth, gently stand her to her feet as I sit down in her place and place her on top of my hard on. I cradle her in my arms gently as I move us in slow thrusts.

"Faster Spencer."

"No." As I kiss her neck and shoulders whilst keeping her in the hold. She tries to quicken the pace as she places her feet firmly on the shower floor. I reach for them and place them round my waist and fold her feet behind me as I carry on slowly rocking us.

"Spencer." She says as she tries to kiss me but her lips are too sore and re opens the split. She places her head in the crease of my neck and shoulder and holds me tight with her one arm. I rock us a little faster as she unravels around me. She milks me for what feels an eternity as I empty myself inside of her.

"You didn't ask me. Why?"

"I know." Holding her tight. "I didn't want to break the connection." we sit there and just be with each other in the embrace we started in. After I re showered her and myself we dressed and laid there on the bed for a while.

"Why did you follow me when I left? I thought you just left me and never gave me a second thought." She laid there stroking my chest.

"I always kept tabs on you Lenny. I didn't follow you at first. I had word on what you were doing. It was a few years in when our paths first crossed. I couldn't breathe when I came across you. I wanted so bad to tell you what you were getting stuck in. I even dropped messages around to give the heads up without you knowing it was me but you never took any notice. WHY Lenny WHY?"

"I thought someone was messing around with us. Playing jokes or being stupid. I didn't want to believe it I guess. The more it became apparent that it wasn't a joke or wind-up I was intrigued on what was actually happening so we stuck around and tried to get in deeper so we could expose what we were seeing. We tried but no one would either listen or they were on the pay role. By the time we tried to get out it was too late."

"Shit. So I made you go in deeper. Fuck Lenny." I jump up off the bed and start pacing, "You are telling me I tried warning you and it made you want to know more. Get involved more Put you in even more danger. Go in deeper. What you telling me is I nearly had you killed? FUCK!"

"Spencer. It doesn't matter. We can say all about the What If's and so on but it doesn't make any difference."

"No difference! You're joking me right. I tried getting you out of there and what I actually did is push you further in. Lenny I NEARLY GOT YOU KILLED!" I leaned right over her small frame. "KILLED LENNY. FUCKING

KILLED! How am I supposed to live with myself knowing that the one person I love more than anything in this life I nearly had MURDERED!"

"Now THAT'S a little extreme even for you Spencer. I wasn't in any danger really. Especially having you there."

"The point is Lenny. YOU DIDN'T KNOW I was there till I just told you! Jesus Lenny what if you had died." Standing in the middle of the room, feeling lost I stare at Lenny shaking from head to foot. "What if we didn't get to you in time Lenny?" I whispered "What if.." she leapt off the bed and flung herself on me.

"But you did Spencer. You did. You, as it seems, have controlled my life for many years and I, for one, not knowing it was you pulling the strings. I am the one who should be pissed right now Spencer not you. We have both made choices that we need to live within our lives and now isn't the time to hang them out on the line. This conversation can wait."

"No Lenny it can't!"

"Yes Spencer it can. We are both angry with what is happening at the minute and this needs to end before THIS conversation can come to a close. Now I can hear the wagon coming. Let's go and sort the animals out and revisit this at another time." With that she walks out of the bedroom and heads downstairs.

"Lenny wait for me." As I chase behind her.

Chapter 47.

Lennox.

The pain I feel in my head is unbearable but I need to focus on the job at hand. I will revisit this fight with him later. Now isn't the time. The van reverses up the drive and I can see my very own black beauty. The most beautiful face of hands full of calm Friesian horse that I cannot wait to ride. Quickly followed by the hearing of two crazy pigs in the next section. Oh Pinky and Perky seem to be in full volume.

"Hello my beautiful." I say to my beautiful horse as I stroke her nose giving her a sugar cube. Welcome to your new home. Now I know I can't ride you yet but you and I are going to have so much fun when I can." Nodding in agreement with me as if she knew what I was saying.

The driver came round the back. "Hey there. I guess you were expecting these little characters today?" he asks.

"I most certainly am. How was the travel?"

"Not too bad. They have had food and water today and the journey wasn't too rough so they're content enough. Shall we release the hounds as they say?"

"Yes, let's shall we."

"You may want to stand back a little you don't look too good. That looks like one hell of a fall or fight you have had!" Smiles at me as he opens the back.

Pip's all angst. "It's alright girl just a few more friends." As I stroke her head. "Come on girl." I walk her away from the van. She wouldn't move and showing her teeth. "What's wrong Pip?" As the man behind me cocks a gun behind my head.

"Move. Now!"

"Where?" I ask trying not to show I am scared.

"In the house go!"

I make my way to the house as Pip runs off.

"What do you want from me?"

"The drive WHERE IS IT?"

"For fuck sake not this AGAIN!" I yell "Go find it yourself. Anyway MI5 have a copy so your too late!"

"Nice try. Where is it?"

"MI5 has it."

"AGAIN. STOP LYING! Where is it?" As he pushes me down onto the window seat. His back to the door. Rookie mistake. "I don't have it MI5 does. "

"That's where you're wrong. It only had Johnson's take on things and what he has done. Nothing about the rest of the operation."

"What operation is that then?"

"You know exactly what operation!"

"That's where you're wrong. I have no Idea arsehole."

"You have already gone a few rounds. I can always make you're war wounds a lot worse. Now tell me WHERE IS THE ORIGINAL?"

"Right here!" Spencer says just as he cracks his head with the handle of his gun.

"Come here Pip. You clever girl." As I kiss her as much as I can as she licks me like a lollipop on a Summers day.

"Fuck sake Spencer. How many more goons are they going to send?"

"He is a hired hit."

"How do you know?"

"This." Pulling orders out of his back pocket.

"But let's be sure shall we! We need to tie him up. I only have one pair of cuffs left the rest went last night."

"Oh hang on." As I run upstairs. "Will this help?" With a wink.

"Nicely!" We attach his hands and feet to the spreader pinning him to a chair. "SMILE!" Spencer says as we take a picture off his phone and send it to his contacts. Two as it seems. "Just for good measure!" I tell him. "You never know who's watching!"

"Who sent you?" Spencer asks. Nothing.

"I said. Who sent you?" As he hits him across his face. "Just tell me who sent you. And before you say Johnson it's not going to stick we already have him so you may as well spill." Nothing.

"No matter. We have sent your little selfie out to your contacts I am sure we will find out soon enough. Squirming in his seat trying to get out of the restraints.

"Fuss as much as you like you won't get out of it, WHO SENT YOU?" SMACK, another hit when Spencer's phone rings.

"Yes. Back door." He says,

"Lucky for you your lift has arrived. Hope you enjoy your new living quarters. I hear it's MI5 have a lovely cells available. Don't forget to say hello Fraydo when you get there. Him and I go waaaaaaay back." As Spencer moves him finger across his throat. You can see the fear in his eyes sitting there knowing what's ahead of him is way scarier than what's in front of him now. As Zaff and Nibble walk in to collect our new friend.

"Errr any chance of leaving the restraints behind?" I ask laughing. "Honestly Spencer. Will this shit ever end?" I cuddle in to him as he simply picks me up and carries me upstairs and lays us on the bed. The next thing I know my eyes close and drift off to sleep.

Chapter 48.

Spencer.

"What on earth." I jump out of my sleep. "There it is again." As I hear a ruckus outside."That fucking goat. Houdini I am selling you to market tomorrow!" I mumble to myself as I put my jeans on and head outside. This goat will be the end of me. He is definitely going to the butchers. Walking down the stairs I also hear Pip growling.

"What's wrong girl? Houdini winding you up too is he?" Bolting out of the door as soon as I open it to give her a stroke. "Well there's no need for that girl." As I walk over to corner Houdini always ends up at. Not there. "Where the hell are you goat?" I head over to the wall and use the light off my phone to see the porch. Not there. "What the hell?" As I hear him behind me. "I swear goat you are one nightmare!" As I see him in his pen. "How on earth did you get back in there?" I say as I hear Pip whimper. "Pip, what's wrong girl, where are you?" I see she is laying on the mat blood coming from her. "What's happened girl?" Realisation setting in. "LENNYYYYYY!" I shout rushing into the house. No sign of her. I run around the house searching and searching. I pull the feed up on my phone. He has disconnected the live feed. "FUCK!" running my hands through my hair "FUCK. THINK. THINK. THINK!" Hitting my forehead with the palm of my hand. My blood runs cold seeing a blood trail on the floor. I follow it leading outside. Pip still on the floor whimpering, I ring Nibble.

"Send reinforcements Lenny has been lifted. There's blood trail in the house she is here somewhere get here now!" I follow the blood trail and leads up the gravel path. "Hold on baby. I am coming." I say to myself as I keep following the splatter. I can hear shuffling ahead of me.

"How do I get in it Lennox? Open it Lennox NOW!" I hear him shouting at her.

"NO. It isn't hear I don't have it anymore. Your too late!"

"Nice try. How do I get into Lennox. Show me!"

"FUCK OFF!"

"You think this dress up of your gargoyle was just for kicks? I know it is to put people off the scent of where it is and what secret it holds. Hiding it in plain sight"

"What are you talking about?"

"Gordo. Your secret teller and keeper! We all know you tell him your secrets. What better place to keep them safe eh? WHERE IS IT?"

"You're delusional if you think that is anything more than a statue. Gordo is a gargoyle, a statue how on earth can I put something there? Get a grip you idiot! I don't have whatever it is you think I have now let me go!" Lenny notices I am right there mouthing sorry to me. My heart is breaking. How did it end up like this.

Forcing her onto her knees pointing a gun to her head. "You have five seconds to tell me!"

"Or what? You will shoot me? Well I won't be any use to you then will I DEAD. What an absolute moron!"

"I didn't say I would kill you. Well not yet anyway. I will start with a few flesh wounds first then work my way though a few little cuts here and there. Don't underestimate my capabilities Lennox. Now TELL ME!"

I nod to her letting her know to give him the drive.

"FINE. There a loose section of concrete under the back of his neck. It is in there."

Topez drags her to her feet. "You get it. No tricks."

"Jesus calm your shit down!"

"Mouthpiece just DO IT!"

Lenny moves all the dress up away and takes away the concrete and puts her arm down the hollow section and pulls out the drive "HERE." Throws it to the ground and Banner runs to pick it up.

"Let her go Topez. Games over. MI5 are on route and your finished!" Pointing my gun at him. He turns as he stays pointing the gun to Lenny's head.

"I don't think so Stone. I haven't come this far to just walk away. I want what's mine."

"Why you don't need it anymore. The games up. It is already at MI5. They know it all and are after YOU now. You have nowhere else to go. Your organisation is finished. Pretty smart putting Johnson in the front line. We all knew it wasn't him. You fucked up there."

"How did you know?"

"When Crystal beat your face to a pulp the night of the party. You really do need to be more careful bugging places."

"What do you mean Crystal?"

"We swapped Lenny for Crystal knowing you were going to attempt to lift her. If you came to the party and attempted we would mark you so we knew once and for all and low and behold the next day you had a shiner. Only one person gives those beauties out. Our suspicions were correct. You always showed up at times to stop them lifting her as you still didn't know for sure if she had the drive. You played the long game. I had my suspicions when you wormed your way in to my crew after the forest. Only one reason for that was to have a little bit of us, watching her, watching you and that gave us the information we knew all along. We needed you in play so we could take down the whole organisation but we could only do that with the drive. The only problem was. We didn't know if Lenny had it still. So you stayed on board to make sure your operation was still in business without getting your hands dirty and not getting caught out. But what you have there isn't your precious organisation. As she said MI5 has it!"

"Nice try Stone. Even I know you don't trust them. I think you have forgotten the shit they put you through with them all on the take. You don't deal with them anymore and they certainly won't be heading your way. You aren't the only one with skills Stone. Bailey isn't who you think he is either!"

"That's where you're wrong Topez or should we say Banner? I am exactly who he thinks I am!" Bailey says pointing his gun at him. "You are surrounded Topez. Games up. You don't think Johnson went to you by accident do you? We knew he was dirty and on the take. The only reason he came and worked as your informant was because he was ours. We knew his game and was caught out. We needed someone on the inside and he proved invaluable. His only problem was he then thought he was above everybody. Wrong. He gave the impression I was on the wrong side simply to put you off the scent. THIS" he said pointing to myself and him, "All of this? Mine and Stones operation. Not Johnsons, not yours, OURS. Now put your gun down and lay on the ground!"

"What? HOW?"

"CRYSTAL! Oh yes. Did you miss that bit Topez?" I say. "This plan has been in our total control for three years. Crystal put us onto you after the night we saved Lenny. It wasn't by chance she dragged me to safety. She had seen you pushing your weight around in your operations, gathered her own evidence over time but still wasn't enough. She needed help and we were it. You're finished PUT THE GUN DOWN AND GET ON THE GROUND!"

"CRYSTAL?" He says staring at the ground trying to connect all the dots. "How did I miss that?"

"DOWN ON THE GROUND TOPEZ NOW!"

"NO!" As he cocks the gun to Lenny.

"NOW LENNY!" as she rolls away, Topez fires as I take the shot and Topez hits the ground. I run to Lenny and hold her. "Pip's injured I need to get to Pip." she cries.

"We need a vet Pip's hurt," I say to Bailey as we start to run back up to the house. There's no sign of her when we reach the house.

"Where can she be Spencer?" Lenny starts to cry

"PIIIIIP," she shouts as we hear a little whimper from inside the house. We run inside and she laying on the window seat, shaking and cold. I grab a blanket from the back of the seat wrap her up and run to the car with Lenny behind me.

"Maddox. There's been an incident and Pip's been hurt. Can you ring Jane and meet us at the practice. We will be there in five."

"What we looking at?"

"I think a stab wound to the neck. Not sure."

"Will be prepped ready for you."

Pulling up to Maddox's practice he is there at the door running to us, Jane, his practice partner was lining everything up in the room as we rush in.

"Please Maddox. Save her." Lenny pleads with her brother,

"It's alright sis calm down go sit down and let me do my job." Pacing into the waiting area.

"Lenny please come here and sit down. Your making yourself dizzy. She is in safe hands."

"I can't Spencer," she cries. " I am supposed to keep these animals safe and she is dying in there and he won't let me be with her. I need to be with her!"

"Come here." Gathering her up and sit her down on my knee and cradle her. I feel her top saturated. "Babe. Your soaked." as she collapses in my arms.

Chapter 49.

Lennox.

My head is pounding and I can barely open my eyes. I can feel something soft in my hand I half open one eye and see Spencer's head under my hand sleeping.

"Why am I here?" I say to Spencer waking up in a hospital room stroking his hair.

"Your awake. Thank god for that you feeling alright baby?"

"Why am I here. How's Pip?"

"Pip's fine. You gave us all one hell of a scare there."

"What happened to me?"

"You collapsed in the Maddox's vets. I thought it was from everything that happened but you were drenched as it happens a stray bullet actually hit your shoulder but we didn't know till you collapsed. How didn't you feel it?"

"I was shot?"

"Yeah baby you were. Three days ago."

"Three days ago?"

"Yes. You have been out of it since. They needed to operate to get the bullet out." I tell her as I buzz for the Doctor and everybody piles in when they hear the noise. The doctor has to push his way through the crowd to get to her.

"Well Missy. You gave us all a scare there. Next time you get shot please come straight to the hospital. Preferably before you lose too much blood! Can we have the room please?" He says to everybody. "I know you are all relieved she has woken up but I need to check her over. I promise I won't be too long."

"We will be all outside my don't worry." Caitlin says, "We aren't going anywhere." As they all leave.

"Right. Let's check you over shall we. You have certainly been through the wars young lady. At least your wound is the same side as your hand. Take from that what you will." as he laughs. " Right. Your puncture wound will take a while to heal so you need to keep coming back for your dressing to be changed and then you need physiotherapy for about eight weeks to help gain full movement which I am certain you will gain but will take time even after physio. You will need a lot of help in the meantime and afterwards. You cannot over strain it and can only use it limited amounts. I hear you have animals. NO mucking out you need help with that as it includes a lot of leaning over and strain. That needs to be done by someone else. I can tell you, however, you can supervise," Winking at me and nods in Spencer's direction, as I smile at him. "There is one other thing I need to address with your blood work," as a nurse comes in with a machine.

"My blood work? Has the bullet poisoned me? You hear about lead poisoning all the time."

"No not lead poisoning. Please can we turn out the lights?" As the nurse turns off the lights and plugs in the machine. "Something came apparent in the operation."

"What's going on Doctor?" I ask as he puts jelly then the machine onto my torso. Spencer is looking at me worried.

"What's happening Spencer? What's wrong with me?"

Spencer sits down. Holds my hand and cries.

Chapter 50.

Spencer.

"You can go home tomorrow all being well. Try and rest and I will call back this evening before I leave."

"Thanks doctor." I shake his hand and follow him out.

"You can all come back in now." As they all pile in. I stand there at the door and watch them all sit round her. She looks at me with tears in her eyes.

"I will be back soon. I have a few things I need to do and will go and grab you some fresh clothes and wash bag." I turn and leave. I find my car and drive home and I can't do anything else but cry.

I park up in the car park of work, go straight to the dressing room change into my workout gear and head for the bags. People must notice I aren't in any mood to be nice and move away from me as I go to town on the bags. I fight the bag for thirty minutes straight till my arms are numb. I head for the shower wash and change and head home. Not speaking to anyone. I go to Lenny's first and put some clothes together and a wash bag with her favourites products and then jump over the wall to mine where I find mam and dad sat on the veranda.

"Hey son." Dad says as mam comes and throws her arms around me.

"How is she doing son? How are YOU holding up?"

"I nearly got her killed dad. I nearly got her killed." I stand there holding mam and cry again.

"The point is son. You saved her."

"I nearly got her killed. She means EVERYTHING to me and I nearly got her killed. She got beat up, held at gun point and shot all because of me!"

"No. It isn't because of you. It was because of those other bastards. You were there every step of the way keeping her safe. You brought her home to keep her safe. You kept her close to keep her safe and you did!" Dad tells me.

"Yes I know I did dad but I also put her in harm's way and she nearly paid the ultimate price for that."

"But she didn't and THAT is what's important here."

"I should have just made her give me the damn drive years ago and this would have been prevented."

"You needed this to happen son. This was the only way and you know it."

"Yes but she wasn't meant to get hurt I nearly lost everything. My family everything I ever wanted I nearly lost. For what?"

"For bringing an end to one of the biggest smuggling operations known to man. You have just brought down an organisation of drug smuggling, animal cruelty, rare species ring and whatever else they find. A lot of people sleep better tonight knowing they are safe and that's on you and YOUR organisation. Lenny being part of it without her knowing maybe a good thing or a bad thing we will never know but one thing for sure is you got her home to safety and that's all that matters."

"She's pregnant."

"Pardon?" Mam and dad say together.

"She's pregnant. Only early stages but I nearly lost her and our baby. How do I forgive myself for that as I don't think I ever will and I don't think Lenny will either."

"I am going to have a grandchild?" mams says crying, it's a watershed at mine at the minute I swear if there was a drought it would now be over.

"Yeah mam you are. The problem is they had to put her under to operate. Now, he said things will more than likely be alright. She will need extra checks to see how the pregnancy progresses but they're not out of the woods yet." As I get crushed in between the both of them.

We sit and talk a few more minutes before I tell them I need to go back to the hospital I just needed to pick a few things up. I say goodbye and head back.

I walk back into the hospital room and it is in full swing of laughter. I plonk our bags in a corner kiss her head and sit next to her on the bed.

"How did the opening go? Can't believe I missed it."

"We postponed it. We open this weekend instead." Jameson answers,

"Oh great that means I won't miss it. But why did you postpone it?"

"Well with you all shot and broke, very selfish of you indeed, we didn't want you to miss it so we cancelled it till this week but all good now."

"Ahhhh, what a gorgeous brother you are." She tells him "But open those doors and get the customers in." she tells him as she yawns her little head off.

"Right guys I think that's your queue to leave. I will keep you updated so keep you're phones on." They all take a turn to kiss her goodbye and leave.

"Thank you bro for saving my girl," she tells Maddox. "Anytime little sis, she is fine and at home with me don't worry now sleep and get better. We have a party to go to at the weekend." He kisses her forehead laughs and leaves and I lay on the bed next to her.

"How you feeling Baby?"

"Numb. You?"

"Emotional." I can't lie to her. Not anymore.

"I love you Lenny. You scared the fucken shit out of me. I nearly got you killed I will never forgive myself for that and now we learn I could have killed our baby too I can't wrap my head around it I nearly lost..." She turns my head and kisses me.

"Stop. It's over and done with. We are all fine and safe."

"Safe! I nearly got you killed are you not listening to me."

"Spencer. I love you with my whole heart but will you please shut up so I can go to sleep."

"You love me?"

She puts her fingers to my lips "SHHHHHHHHH." and doses off. I watch her sleep for what feels like an eternity as I take out her ring and place it on her finger and I fall asleep next to her. Next thing we know the Doctor is coming back in and checking her vitals as we both wake up.

"Sorry." He says, "I didn't mean to wake you. I am heading out and doing my last checks. All of your appointments are booked in." as he hands me her appointment booklet. "If you are well enough I will let you go home on Wednesday. We are just making sure ALL of you are alright before we let you leave. I will be back in the morning. Until then rest." Looking at her finger, laughs and walks out.

"Spencer."

"Yes babe?"

"What day is it?"

"Monday."

"Spencer."

"Yes babe?"

"How long have I been in here for?"

"Three days babe."

"Spencer."

"Yes babe?"

"What is this doing on my finger?" Lifting her left hand and shows me the red, plastic ring I won her when we were kids out of a penny machine and told her one day I would propose to her with it.

"I thought it was time you wore it so people know your mine."

"Ah right. So me being pregnant isn't a part of this then?"

"Naaaaah. The ring came first, who knows how the baby landed in there?"

"Spencer."

"Yes babe?"

"I love you."

"Lenny."

"Yes babe?"

"Do you like it."

"Yeah it's perfect."

"Lenny."

"Yes babe?"

"I can always get you another one if you think it is too old."

"No it's perfect."

"Lenny."

"Yes babe?"

"I love you too."

"Lenny."

"For fuck sake Yes Babe?"

"Shut up and kiss me."

"Ah come here then." As she turns and kisses me like never before.

Chapter 51.
Epilogue.
Finally been home a few days, camera and bug free and with my animals. Spencer has been nothing but a fuss pot and doing my head in, however, he has been a darling and looked after the animals for me. Obviously I have been supervising WHEN he has let me move that is. Pip stays right next to me with an ice cream cone on her head. She walks in the house no problem. I feel it has to do with her saving me the way she did. She saw Topez coming for me with a knife and she tried to bite him, he swung and caught her neck but she is nearly as good as new if not better now she is brave to come inside. In fact we have made her a bed area inside so she doesn't have to stay in the outside pen anymore. She much rather prefers inside now than out. Black Beauty has settled in even though she had a rocky start and the pigs have enough mud to lay in so they're great. Houdini and pal have been moved into the spare horse paddock so he

can't escape anymore which they seem happier about as a little bit more space is always a good thing. Tomorrow night is opening night and I cannot wait. I promised I would be good and not leave the booth but I am most definitely attending. I hear Spencer coming in after his morning rounds whilst I laid on the window seat and watched his gorgeous arse out in the garden.

"Pudding?"

"Custard?"

"I was thinking."

"Well ring the fire brigade your brains on fire."

"Ha. Ha. Chubbers."

"Fuck off Dipstick." I can't help laughing at him.

"When do you want to tell the group about the baby? Also, can you tell me why didn't it even occur to either one of us to use protection? How can we have been so stupid?"

"I guess my birth control ran out. I guess with everything going on I must have needed a booster and forgotten about it or it just didn't work, either way I am so sorry. I know this wasn't in either one of our plans right now and I understand if you want to walk but this baby is staying."

"Wooooo there horsey. I aren't going anywhere and I am STOKED that we are having a baby. I just can't believe it has happened. You hated me two months ago and since then I have bugged your house, had you followed, kidnapped, thrown out of a window, slashed, shot, impregnated and engaged. It's been a busy time for me. I have invested a lot already in this relationship I aren't walking after all of that effort I have put in. Are you mad woman?" As I spit my water I just drank all over the room in hysterical laughter.

"Yes that is a lot to pile into a relationship in just two months, I dread to think what the next two have in store. What else are you planning?" Leaning in for a kiss.

"Well that will be telling won't it. So back to my original question. When do we tell the guys?"

"Heeeey there holy. How's my bud doing?" Caitlin shouts as she comes in for a visit. "Tell us guys what? As she stands there with cakes in one hand and the other on her hip.

"Easy tiger. Want a drink?"

"Yeah coffee please but I can do it. Tell us what?"

"Not a chance. He won't let me move a finger and I am going stiff. I can't wait for tomorrow night." pointing to Spencer,

"Oh is he letting you go is he?" Laughing

"Nothing to do with him. I am totally going." I say smiling at him as he sits on the window seat stroking Pip.

"GOOD." As she winks at me "Now tell the guys what? What's the winking for? What's going on?"

"Shall we tell her and swear her to secrecy? Hang on just a minute." I say " I know that look. What are you up to Cait's?"

"You tell me yours and I will tell you mine!"

"No way Cait's you first."

"Well! You know the drummer from Blackout?"

"Yeah. Sort of. Met him at the party. What about him?"

"Well. Because we put the opening on hold for a week the band went away skiing for a few days and he fell and broke a few bones."

"Ah one of your guys baby." Spencer remarks.

"Oh my days never! So can't they perform? What are we going to do? Shit. Does Jameson know? Do we need to find another band?" Caitlin just stands there with a great big smile on her face.

"Calm down there Ritalin. They have a stand in." She says with a cheesy smile.

"Alright. I will bite. Who's the stand in?" As she shows me a picture.

"NO WAY!" I sat mouth open which quickly changes to a great big grin.

"Who?" Spence asks,

"This is going to be fun. But I thought motor cross was the dream not the band?"

"WHO?" he asks again,

"I guess you help out friends where you can. A bit like scratching an itch." laughing at me.

"Fuck sake will you answer me WHO? Jesus I am turning into a woman!" he says burying his head in his hands then walking over to us.

"Oh this is going to be REAL GOOD!"

"Will SOMEONE tell me WHO ALREADY!"

"Isn't it just. And Jameson still doesn't know?"

"Nope. He knows the drummer is out of action and they have a stand in just not who."

"Oh I can't wait for this." As we sit drink and talk about old times.

"PLEASE I AM BEGGING YOU. WHO IS THE DRUMMER?" Caitlin turns the picture she has on her phone to show him and smiling.

"Oh boy. You're right. This IS going to be good. I can't wait. I am having front row seats to this show down!"

"ERRRR never mind show down. What is it you are contemplating telling us?"

We look at each other. "This goes nowhere. Promise us Caitlin. Not till the groups altogether."

"You're scaring me. Is this about the baby. Are you both alright?"

Shocked. we both look at her stunned. "How?" We both say together.

"We all had our ears to the door when the Dr ordered us out and the nurse came in with the machine. We are all waiting for you to both to tell us. I AM SOOOOO FREAKING EXCITED RIGHT NOW!" as she puts her coffee down and throws herself at us.

"So you all know?"

"Yeah we do. They're just waiting for you tell them officially and will you hurry up because they're bursting with excitement."

"You ALL know?" Spencer asks again.

"YES. ALL KNOW. What do you not understand about that sentence?"

"Ohhh. You thinking what I am thinking?" Spencer asks me.

"Maybe. What is it you're thinking?"

"NO! NO! NO! NO! NO!" Caitlin points at us with a grin. "No more secrets. Look what happened the last time!"

"Oh Yes. Secret till they squirm?"

"Oh Yes!" As we high five.

"Ah Maaaaaan." Caitlin says shakes her head.

Chapter 52.

Jameson.

JAMMY: HOLY. I know you're on supervisory duties but I have been caught up on a job. Can you go and let the band in so they can set up please. I wouldn't ask if I wasn't desperate. Caitlin is on her way there now could you possible meet her there? (Praying emoji)

ME: I am over the road in the cafe with Spencer. I will bring food.

JAMMY: Sis you are a life saver. Stop eating all the cakes you will get fat. Something you want to tell me porky?

ME: Shut up Fun Boy Three. . Do you want me to let Caitlin in or not? :P

JAMMY: Sorry. I will bring you more cake now GO! GO! GO!

ME: It ain't what you do it's the way that you do it :D

JAMMY: I hate you (Angry emoji)

ME: I love you too. See you later

I can't believe the brewery have sent the wrong order to PAP's again I need to change breweries, they're just aren't good enough. The last thing I need today is this. The band has a stand in drummer because they're a man down. Thank goodness as I wouldn't have another band to replace them and the DJ is still away but they're good to go. Just bad business not being able to be there to greet them. Good job they know the family from the party. As I head into PAP's the bar manager is there.

"Sorry boss. Look that's the order sent. This is what they're bringing. I swear they are taking the piss!" Gino says,

"Don't worry. I know it wasn't you. Let's get this shit sorted shall we. We are on opening night tonight so I need to be over at Boyo's."

"On it boss." as Gino and myself go to brewery war.

It's a little past six by the time I get sorted.

ME: Thanks for helping today bud. Just got home did the band get sorted alright?

CAIT: All sorted Terry Hall. Sound check went well and doing another later so See you at opening :D

ME: Great. See you soon

I head home for a quick shower and dress change and head over to the bar. I open up and let myself in. Turn on all the pumps and lights as the gang walk in.

"Hey you are all on time. Besides you Lenny you sit you're arse down. Let's get opened up shall we."

The bar staff come in and Gino has even came across to make sure they all know what they're doing. He is a marvel. PAP's he has as a well oiled machine and he will go back over tonight when it opens for the nightclub. He puts the staff to work. I head into the kitchen were the staff are already preparing for this evenings events. I have a two sectioned kitchen. VIP's and their food orders already taken in advance and are being prepped on one side and the other side of the kitchen for on the spot orders. Making sure they have everything in order I hear the band in sound check. As I head out and make my way over to them all I can hear is them all laughing and joking. I stand back and just enjoy the sight. It has been such a long time since we were altogether and this happy.

"Hey, sounds like there's fun to be had over here. What's so.." As I stop dead in my tracks and see red.

"Jameson. Long time."

"Gina. Not long enough!"

Acknowledgments.

Where do I begin? To AnneMarie and Liz for forcing me to write the book in the first place, after wanting to for so long and giving me the confidence to accomplish my dream. With an immense THANK YOU to my very own secret reading book club, whom I could never have made it this far without. Your support in all areas of this book, especially the proof reading, note making, re reading, helped me make it to the end. We are the perfect team. Our secret book club lives on girls. Also, AMW for the fabulous front cover.

And to you dear readers. I hope you enjoyed Spencer and Lennox. They were an absolute joy to write. They just came alive on paper and I truly hope you enjoyed their story as much I did writing it.

Thank you to everyone who has brought Whitesands Elite alive and into the world.

ALSO BY TILLY.

JAMESON.

MADDOX.

CAITLIN.

DONNY.

JAXON.

WHITESANDS FINALE.

Printed in Great Britain
by Amazon